SECOND CHANCE UNDER THE MISTLETOE

KANDY SHEPHERD

Harlequin
ROMANCE

H Harlequin®
ROMANCE

ISBN-13: 978-1-335-47061-4

Second Chance Under the Mistletoe

Recycling programs
for this product may
not exist in your area.

Harlequin Enterprises ULC
22 Adelaide St. West, 41st Floor
Toronto, Ontario M5H 4E3, Canada
www.Harlequin.com

HarperCollins Publishers
Macken House, 39/40 Mayor Street Uppe
Dublin 1, D01 C9W8, Ireland
www.HarperCollins.com

Printed in U.S.A.

Family Reunion in London

Fairy lights and fairy tale romance...

The Grayson family's Christmas is destined to be very cold indeed. Parents Jon and Natalie are estranged—and living on different continents—while daughter Clem has just found out that she's pregnant, with no dad on the scene! But with a sprinkle of Christmas magic, everything is about to change...

Curl up by the fire with a mug of hot chocolate, and get swept away by this gorgeous wintry duet!

Follow Jon and Natalie's romantic reunion in

Second Chance Under the Mistletoe
by Kandy Shepherd

And Clem's workplace romance with Leo in

Christmas Surprise for Her Boss
by Scarlet Wilson

Both available now!

Dear Reader,

Do you enjoy a second-chance romance as much as I do? I love the idea of going back to a relationship that didn't work out the first time with the hope that, this time, true love might bloom.

In *Second Chance Under the Mistletoe*, Natalie and Jon first met as teenagers and their passionate first love felt like forever love. However, life got in the way. They parted in bitterness to live on opposite sides of the world—but not before having a beautiful daughter, Clementine.

More than twenty years later, Clementine brings her parents together for a Christmas reunion. It's only with great reluctance Natalie and Jon agree to attend. Unresolved pain and emotion are still there, but the old attraction is just a spark away from rekindling. Can a touch of Christmas magic help them open up to a second chance at love—this time for a well-deserved happy-ever-after?

Second Chance Under the Mistletoe is part of the Family Reunion in London duet. Watch out for Clementine's story, *Christmas Surprise for Her Boss*, by Scarlet Wilson.

Kandy Shepherd

Kandy Shepherd swapped a career as a magazine editor for a life writing romance. She lives on a small farm in the Blue Mountains near Sydney, Australia, with her husband, daughter and lots of pets. She believes in love at first sight and real-life romance—they worked for her! Kandy loves to hear from her readers. Visit her at kandyshepherd.com.

Books by Kandy Shepherd

Harlequin Romance

The Christmas Pact

Mistletoe Magic in Tahiti

Christmas at the Harrington Park Hotel

Their Royal Baby Gift

How to Make a Wedding

From Bridal Designer to Bride

One Year to Wed

Cinderella and the Tycoon Next Door

Second Chance with the Single Dad
Falling for the Secret Princess
One Night with Her Millionaire Boss
Second Chance with His Cinderella
Pregnancy Shock for the Greek Billionaire
The Tycoon's Christmas Dating Deal

Visit the Author Profile page
at Harlequin.com for more titles.

To Lucy, my wonderful daughter

Praise for
Kandy Shepherd

CHAPTER ONE

IF THERE WAS one person Natalie Gibbs loved more than anyone in the entire universe, it was her daughter, Clementine. She'd given birth to her when she'd been nineteen years old and, in many ways, her life still centred around her. That wasn't to say that sometimes her only child didn't exasperate her to the point of gritted teeth. Now was just such a moment.

She sat opposite Clem at a Tudor-inspired café in her home town of Guildford, Surrey. Twenty-four-year-old Clem had invited her to lunch, a lovely surprise when her darling daughter now lived in central London. Yet Clem was hedging around the reason for the meeting. And Natalie knew her daughter didn't like to be pushed. She wished she would just come out with it. Clem had dropped a baby bombshell on her back in July. Whatever she might hit her with today couldn't be as momentous as that news of an unplanned pregnancy.

With Christmas only three weeks away, the town was decked out for the festive season. Mother and daughter chatted about how wonderful the lights looked along the historic, cobbled high street. How impressive the tree was in the main shopping mall. How sorry Clem had been to miss the Christmas market this year. How pleased Natalie was to be able to get all her Christmas shopping done without having to leave her home town. Both she and Clem agreed that Christmas simply wouldn't be Christmas without the constant playing of 'Deck the Halls with Boughs of Holly' and 'All I Want for Christmas Is You' piped into seemingly every space—even though it could get annoying.

Finally, they exhausted the festive small talk. An awkward silence fell between them. Natalie took a sip of tea, then put down her cup. After what seemed like an age, Clem leaned across the table closer to Natalie. Natalie noted her daughter took a deep breath before she spoke, then followed it out with a rush of words.

'Mum, I want to have Dad with us on Christmas Day.'

Immediately Natalie felt awash in a wave of sadness. Her husband, Hugo Gibbs, had died almost two years ago. He'd been the best possible stepfather to Clem and her daughter had adored him.

She reached out to grip Clem's hand. 'Of course you do, sweet pea. I miss him too. This will only be our second Christmas without him and—'

'No, Mum, you don't understand. I mean I want to invite my birth father to have Christmas with us.'

Natalie withdrew her hand. 'Wh…what do you mean?'

'I've invited Jonathan Grayson to lunch on Christmas Day. My biological father.' She paused. 'You know, your first husband.'

'What?'

Natalie had met Jonathan Grayson, a year older than her, during her first year at university—at freshers' week to be exact. She'd lost her virginity to him on their first date and plunged straight into a tempest of exhilarating, passionate love. She hadn't been able to get enough of him. He'd felt the same about her. They hadn't thought further than the next opportunity to make love. Until she'd fallen pregnant halfway through their second term. He'd pledged to stand by her. But both sets of parents had made it difficult. Angry accusations of educations derailed and bright futures ruined, not to mention family disgrace, had been hurled at them from both sides.

The teenagers had been coerced by Natalie's conservative parents into a hasty, register office wedding. Then, because of lack of funds, had found themselves and a newborn baby living under the roof of those same disapproving parents. It hadn't been easy for Natalie. And certainly not for Jon. Her parents had been openly hostile to him, for no discernible reason other than he'd ruined their plans for how they'd intended their daughter to live her life.

When her new husband had been offered the chance of a well-paying job in the mines of Western Australia, he and Natalie had agreed he should take it. It had been a joint decision, although, looking back, she realised she'd been in no fit condition health-wise to make such a decision. But at the time it had seemed the only way out. He was supposed to come back with enough money for him, Natalie and baby Clementine to find a place of their own. Only he hadn't come back.

It took Natalie a very long moment to find her voice again. 'What do you mean, you've invited your dad for Christmas?'

'I've never spent Christmas with him. I want to this year. He really wants to see me as well, and—'

Natalie put up her hand. 'Wait. But you never see him. You stopped your yearly visitations with him when you were thirteen.'

'Yeah. I know. Back then, he was, in truth, a stranger to me. I'd only ever seen him a few times in my entire life. When you married Hugo, continuing the idea of him being a part of my life seemed disloyal to the man who loved me like a real father. And you know Hugo didn't like me seeing Dad.'

Or *me* seeing Jon, Natalie thought. Hugo had been a haven of security after Jon had left her and Clementine on their own. Turned out he'd cheated on her over there in Australia. Obviously thought he'd get away with it, being so far away. But even in the outback of Australia there had been someone who knew him, knew her, and had let her know what was going on.

At the time of the divorce, she'd been so hurt and angry with Jon that she'd told him—no, screamed at him—that she never wanted to see him again. When she'd started dating him, Hugo had been more than happy about that. And she'd been so grateful to Hugo for the safety net he'd offered her she'd gone along with his request that she didn't change her mind about having no contact with Clementine's father. Communication had all been through her lawyer. Hugo, her fiancé by that point, had handled the handovers of Clem to Jon for visitations at the times when her ex-husband had been back in England. With Jon living in Australia, those visitations had been infrequent—only once per year—and disruptive, until finally Clem herself had put an end to them after Natalie and Hugo got married.

Natalie hadn't seen Jon for twenty years. *And she didn't want to see him now.* Her heart fluttered in panic at the thought.

'So why are you suddenly in touch with him?' Natalie said.

'He sent condolences on Hugo's death. We mainly picked up from there. Although, you know we did occasionally talk on the phone after he stopped visiting.'

Jon had sent a card to her too, on the passing of her husband. She had thrown it into the bin, unopened. Not, admittedly, without a twinge of curiosity, but the habit of keeping him out of her life wasn't one she was in any rush to break.

'What do you mean, you "picked up from there"? He still lives in Australia, doesn't he?'

'He has a place in London, as well. Near Waterloo. He's staying there now, as a matter of fact. An apartment in an old hat factory. It's very cool, near theatres, great restaurants, bars. You know he's seriously minted, don't you? A multimillionaire by all accounts. Maybe even a billionaire.'

Did her ex-husband intend to buy her daughter away from her? Bribe her with those millions?

Natalie looked at the slice of lemon drizzle cake on the plate in front of her and had to swallow against the nausea that threatened to overwhelm her. She pushed the plate away.

'Does that mean you've been to his apartment?'

'Yes.'

'You didn't think to tell me about it?'

That Clem had seen Jon without telling her was like the point of a sharp knife twisting into her heart. She prided herself on the open communication between her and her daughter. Yet Clem had been seeing Jon without her knowledge.

'I knew you wouldn't approve.'

'Not approve? Sweet pea, I would never disapprove of you seeing your birth father. That's your right. But why this year, after all this time? Why for Christmas?'

Clem pushed back in her chair to further reveal the lovely swell of her pregnancy. She'd grown bigger since Natalie had last seen her a few weeks ago. Clem patted her bump. 'This. Genes. Possible inherited traits. I know about the baby's father's side. I know all about your side, but I didn't know about my father's side. I wanted to know more about my baby's grand-father and where my baby will fit in with the Graysons. I had all sorts of questions for Dad.'

'Well, you knew already you have Jon's green eyes.'

Clem smiled. 'And your red hair.'

The best of both of us. That was what Jon had said when she was born.

'But I needed to know more than eye co-lour,' Clem said.

When Clem had informed her she was preg-nant, Natalie had been shocked. And more than a little upset with her daughter for let-ting history repeat itself, although she'd tried not to show it. Hadn't she cautioned her again and again about using reliable contraception? About living her own life to the full before she became responsible for another?

While giving Clem the contraception talk, she had at the same time reassured her daugh-ter that giving birth to her was the best thing she'd ever done. Natalie had never had even the slightest regret about keeping her baby—even in that hellish time living with her parents. She didn't want Clem to ever think anything other than she'd been wanted and loved.

Her annoyance had soon been eclipsed by her joyful anticipation of her grandchild. Thankfully Clem, pregnant at twenty-four, had an excellent degree behind her and a good job with an international bank. Everyone was delighted about the baby. It was so totally different from what Natalie's situation had been.

She'd never had the chance to go back and finish her degree, follow her own career. Rather she'd fallen into managing Hugo's accountancy practice for him. Hardly a career, although she'd done it very well. Just a job. It wasn't until after Hugo died that she'd realised how totally enmeshed her life had become with his—his wants, his needs. And how much more she now, at the age of forty-three, wanted for herself.

'I totally understand why you want to get to know your father—after all, he is your baby's grandfather,' she said. *But why on Christmas Day?*

Sadly—tragically—the baby's father had died. Clem had been in a friends-with-benefits situation with her best friend, Tyler, on and off for six years. Nice though Tyler was, Natalie had wondered to herself over the years if he really was 'the one' for her daughter. She hadn't been surprised when, after a holiday to Rhodes in May with Tyler, Clem had told her they had finally agreed to end their arrangement. Clem hadn't been in love with Tyler that way, and both she and Tyler had felt it was time to look for something real. 'We decided we were better off as just friends—no benefits.'

Sadly, for Tyler, finding true love wasn't to be. Shortly after their return from Rhodes, he had been killed in a car accident. The funeral had been unbearably sad—a young life cut short so prematurely. Tyler's parents had been so grateful that the girl they loved like a daughter was there, Clem hadn't had the heart to tell them what she and Tyler had agreed. Tyler obviously hadn't let them know either that his on-off relationship with Clem had ended. Then, back in July, Clem had phoned Natalie with the bombshell news she was pregnant with Tyler's baby.

The baby was due at the end of January. Her grandchild. And, after her initial shock, Natalie was delighted. She wanted to do everything she could for Clem both before and after the birth. Clem was fiercely independent, but her new boss, Leo Constello, had recently moved in with Clem, so she had some help—for now, at least. Natalie knew they liked each other, but she wasn't sure how serious they were, as Clem was being very cagey. Now she'd decided she also wanted to spend Christmas with both her baby's maternal grandparents.

'Does your get-together with Jon have to be on Christmas Day?' Natalie asked.

Clem jutted out her chin in the stubborn way she'd done since she was a toddler. 'Mum, my baby's father is dead. I know Leo's there, but I need my family with me, too. I've only got you and Dad. I want to have Christmas to make up for all the Christmases I didn't have with him. Dad feels the same.'

'You could have Christmas Eve or Boxing Day with him.'

'I want us all to be together on Christmas Day—my blood family.'

'Why is it so important?'

'Because it's important to me—and to Dad. And, I want you both to meet Leo.'

Natalie wanted to ask why Jon was more important than she was, but of course she didn't. She had never bad-mouthed Jon to her daughter and she wasn't going to start now.

'I see,' she said.

'Do you? Mum, I know your marriage to Dad wasn't great but—'

'I never said that.'

'You didn't have to. Nanna and Pop never had a good word to say about him.'

'Which is one of the reasons we don't see too much of my parents,' Natalie said, tight-lipped.

Clem's face softened. 'I know, Mum, how difficult they can be. You know I've never felt close to them.'

Neither have I, Natalie thought with a shudder. Her brother had always been the favoured one, the golden child, growing up. But she'd pleased her parents by being clever and doing well at school. She'd been artistic and musical too, although they hadn't put much store on those talents. Then had come the great disappointment—the 'whatever-will-the-neighbours-think?' teenage pregnancy.

Fortunately—or sadly, whichever way you'd like to think of it in terms of a family unit—her parents now lived in Spain. They intended to stay in Marbella for Christmas this year to celebrate the festive season with their ex-pat community.

So, it would be just her, Clem, Leo and Jon for Christmas this year. *She couldn't do it.* Her mind raced wildly for alternatives.

'I don't think it would be appropriate to have Jon at our house, do you?' She suspected Jon would also feel uncomfortable about spending Christmas Day in Hugo's house.

Clem nodded. 'Considering that Hugo liked to pretend Dad didn't exist, no I thought I could host Christmas lunch at my place. Do the grown-up thing.'

'Okay,' said Natalie, swallowing her surprise.

Christmas had always been a big deal in their house. Roast turkey with all the trimmings, a flaming pudding, the tree decorated with ornaments collected over the years along with cherished ones made by Clem as a child. When Clem was little, Hugo had dressed up as Santa to Clem's intense delight. Clem had always fiercely resisted any suggestion that Christmas Day would be spent anywhere else but at home.

'You might have to give me a hand cooking the food, although I'll most likely buy it all in. I figured Kensington would be neutral ground,' Clem said.

Clem was right. Clem had moved to London to start a new job after Tyler's death, living in a beautiful period town house that belonged to Clem's wealthy godmother, Audrey, but that

Audrey rarely used. It would be ideal neutral ground for a Christmas celebration.

That was, if Natalie had any intention of showing up there on Christmas Day. She would not be coerced into meeting with her ex-husband—even by the daughter she adored. It would have to be the first Christmas Day ever she would spend without her. Leo, Clem and Jon might be in Kensington, but Natalie would be elsewhere. Exactly where, she didn't know yet. Certainly not Marbella with her parents. Perhaps Toronto with her brother and his Canadian family. Or somewhere she'd never been. Maybe somewhere warm. Africa. India. Anywhere but London where she would be forced into the company of her ex-husband—the thought of which terrified her.

'Mum? Earth to Mum?'

'Oh. Sorry, sweet pea. I was, er, lost in thoughts on what I might help you cook for Christmas.'

'You know the main reason I've started to see Dad? Why I want to see more of him?'

'You said. The genes. Shared DNA. That stuff. I totally understand.'

'That too. But, Mum, I really, really like him. I felt straight away he was family. Maybe it's the blood tie. Or because I'm getting to know him better as an adult. But there's something compelling about him. Some sort of...what's the word? Charisma? Magnetism? Whatever it is, he's got it in spades. You know?'

Natalie nodded, unable to speak. She knew, all right. No one had ever made her feel even a smidgen of how Jon had made her feel. And she'd spent the last twenty years trying to forget it, forget him—for her own sanity's sake.

When this morning his daughter Clementine had told Jon she'd be in Guildford today for lunch with her mother, Jon had immediately got in the car he kept in London—a top-of-the-range German EV sports car—and driven there.

During the hour-long drive, he'd debated with himself the wisdom of such an impulsive move. Clementine hadn't told him where she was meeting Natalie. What exactly did he intend to do when he got to his destination? Search for mother and daughter among the many cafés and coffee shops and introduce himself? Ask if he could join them? Encounter them in the street and pretend it was a coincidence that he should happen to be there, in Guildford, at the same time as they were?

Of course he shouldn't do any of those

things. But he was a private person, used to guarding his feelings. Even a glimpse of how Natalie looked now might make the unconventional family reunion on Christmas Day less awkward. He dreaded the idea of seeing his former wife again for the first time after twenty years, of having to deal with whatever feelings from the past that might evoke, while pretending to be all jolly over Christmas dinner. Not to mention playing it out in front of the daughter he was getting to know and possibly her new boyfriend, if that was what he was. He needed to at least see Natalie beforehand.

Clementine had hinted that Natalie might not react well to her reunion idea. She'd made it quite clear that she wanted to sensitively introduce the topic of Christmas Day with her mother over lunch. She hadn't told Natalie she'd seen Jon since he'd been in England. She'd been worried how her mother would react. Clem's first loyalty was, as it should be, to Natalie. Yet he knew his new-found daughter really wanted the three of them—blood family—to be together on Christmas Day.

'Three and a half of us, actually,' she'd said, smiling as she'd placed a protective hand on her bump. 'Plus, Leo will be joining us.'

Jon had suggested Christmas Eve, or Boxing

Day, the day after Christmas, could work for him but she'd insisted on The Day itself. 'It's not really Christmas if it isn't the twenty-fifth of December,' she'd said firmly. He wondered what Natalie would think about that.

But he had to tread carefully, to let her sort things out with Natalie. He was still virtually a stranger to his daughter. What he really should do now was turn around and head back to London before he reached the outskirts of Guilford.

But he wasn't a person who generally waited around for things to happen. He was unable to resist the opportunity to satisfy his curiosity about the woman he'd never been able to forget. No matter how deeply she'd wounded him by not waiting for him while he'd slogged so hard for their future in the isolated West Australian mines. Or how gutted he'd been that she'd so easily believed false, cooked-up accusations against him of infidelity. The move to Australia had been a sacrifice they'd both been prepared to make—a joint decision freely made. Her demand for a divorce on the grounds of his desertion had come out of the blue. It had been closely followed by an engagement to an older, wealthier man who had taken over as Clementine's father.

It had appeared Natalie wanted more in

terms of wealth and status than Jon had been able to give her. She'd willingly married Hugo Gibbs. Jon sometimes thought her cruel rejection had been behind his own subsequent relentless pursuit of wealth, never stopping, never having enough. But all he'd known at the time was the shocking pain of losing, not only the wife he'd thought was his until death did they part, but also his precious daughter.

Under the terms of the divorce, the court had granted full custody of Clementine to Natalie. Joint custody was impossible because Jon lived in a different country. However, the court had allowed for him to have regular visits with his daughter. In practice, such visitations had proved very difficult, as Natalie had been vehement that her daughter would never, ever be permitted to visit Australia, either alone or accompanied by Jon's mother. In the early years it had been impossible for Jon to afford more than one yearly trip back to England. By the time he could afford the fare to come over more frequently, he'd had difficulty finding the time away from his work that took him to far-flung mines around the world.

Inevitably, his visits to his daughter had never been more than awkward meetings between a stranger and a young child who was understandably nervous around him. He had never seen Natalie, but Hugo, as her fiancé, had always hovered nearby. On paper, Natalie had approved her daughter's contact with her birth father, as such contact was 'in the child's best interest'. But Jon knew she hadn't really wanted him seeing Clementine and had used restricting access as a form of punishment against him. Anger roiled deep in his gut when he thought about it.

Should he get back in his car?

As it turned out, quite by chance, he walked right past the café on the other side of the street where Clem and Natalie were having lunch. Shocked, he stopped—almost skidding on the damp pavement in his surprise. From where he stood, he could clearly see them seated at a table next to the window. They were facing each other and appeared deep in conversation. He was struck by the symbolism of it, mother and daughter snug and cosy inside, father out in the cold on his own.

Natalie. He had missed out on so much by her severing of their marriage. Twenty years later, he still didn't quite know why it had all gone so wrong. Twenty years later the pain was still there, deeply buried but it still hurt if he poked and prodded at it. *You were only kids,* people had said, as if the love and passion and betrayal felt any less because they'd been so young.

He realised he should walk on. But in a padded jacket with the hood up against the icy air, Jon doubted the women would recognise him—even if they took any notice of the tall, broad-shouldered man across the street, stamping his feet against the cold. That was assuming Natalie would even recognise him at all after more than twenty years.

But he recognised her immediately, even from this distance. At forty-three she appeared to be as mesmerisingly beautiful as she'd been the first time he'd first seen Natalie Lewis during freshers' week at Durham University.

He, a second-year engineering student, had been playing guitar and singing at a party at a student house. He'd noticed her watching him, tall, slender, red hair streaming lavishly down her back. She'd started to tap her foot and mouth the words of the song along with him. He'd caught her eye, indicated that she join him. Her eyes had widened, and she'd pointed at her chest. Who, me? she'd mouthed.

He'd nodded, she'd smiled, then joined him. He'd given her a chord and she'd started to sing along with him. They'd been in perfect harmony from the first note, as if they'd sung together many times before. At the end of the three songs to which they'd both known the words, he'd told her she was amazing and spontaneously kissed her on her mouth. After a moment's hesitation she'd kissed him back, then gazed into his face with a quizzical expression that had made him want to kiss her again. So he had.

That had been a longer kiss, a proper kiss, a kiss he hadn't wanted to end. She'd broken away as the kiss had quickly become way too passionate—and not just on his side—considering the circumstances. The other partygoers had clapped and cheered—whether for their singing or their PDA, he hadn't known or cared. When she'd laughed complicitly, her blue eyes gleaming with mischief, he'd known he wanted her as so much more than a singing partner.

He'd asked her out on a date for the next day, even though he'd known he'd have to cancel a prior arrangement with another girl. Turned out Natalie had had to cancel a date too, although he hadn't found that out until later. He'd been utterly and completely smitten with her—and neither of them had dated anyone else after their first date together. At nineteen, he hadn't been able to imagine any other woman in his life—ever.

Now, his ex-wife and daughter got up from the café table. Jon noted how solicitous Natalie was towards their pregnant daughter, Clemmie. He reined in his thought. He had to remember not to call his only child that. It was Clem or Clementine, she'd told him firmly.

He loved his adult daughter, so smart and feisty, so determined to do the right thing by others. But then he'd loved baby Clementine and toddler Clementine, even though he'd only seen her a handful of times, right up to the adolescent Clementine who had decided not to see him at all any more in deference to her new stepfather's feelings. At the time, he'd felt as though his heart had been ripped out. But he'd never stopped loving her, never stopped providing financially for her, never stopped calling her—and he'd lived for those times she'd answered, never stopped hoping that one day she'd want to make him part of her life again. And, deep down, he had never stopped resenting Natalie for believing the worst of him and not sticking with their marriage. He had lost so much. While she had ended up with the jackpot—their daughter.

Jon wanted this new relationship with Clementine to work long-term. He knew he'd need Natalie on board if that was to happen. But would she be willing to allow him even a glimpse into her life now? After all, she'd kept the door firmly shut for more than twenty years. He was being given a second chance to be a father to Clem—and he intended to grab that chance with both hands. He could only hope that the conversation with Clem about Christmas Day went well—at the same time acknowledging that it could equally be a disaster.

What he knew for sure, though, was that it would certainly be a disaster if he was caught here looking like a stalker. Throughout all those years, he had missed contact with Clementine. He didn't want to risk losing the new relationship he now had with her. He knew he should move on. He turned to go.

Then the café door opened and Natalie stood there, flinching at the cold air. Jon stood stock-still, caught his breath and his heart started to pump wildly. He would know her anywhere, even after all this time. The last time he'd seen her was the day before her engagement to Hugo, when he'd begged her not to go through with it. She'd refused, rejecting his plea for reconciliation with disdain and—he'd been shocked to see—hatred for him blazing from her eyes. Now he had to stop himself from staring, from taking in twenty years' worth of change.

She was still Natalie, but lovely in a more mature, elegant way. Her hair—her glorious long hair—was cut much shorter, just skimming her shoulders. She was wearing a well-cut powder-blue coat and long boots. He remembered how she'd liked to wear blue. 'It's what a blue-eyed redhead should wear,' she'd used to say, at the same time smiling at the ridiculousness of following such a rule dictated by fashion magazines. She'd been wearing blue jeans and a bright blue turtleneck the night he'd first met her.

Natalie turned back to help usher Clem out of the door. Then she again faced the street, almost as if she was aware of his gaze on her. Jon quickly averted his eyes, turned on his heel and strode away. His gut churned with sadness and regret for what might have been, what *should* have been. This wasn't the time to introduce himself—he doubted he'd be able to choke out a coherent word. Old scars had been so easily ripped open he wondered if they had ever really healed.

He fought the temptation to look back for another glimpse of his ex-wife, his first love, the woman he'd so naïvely believed would grow old beside him. He had never planned to see her again—not after the way she'd treated him. He'd built a successful life without her, although happiness in relationships continued to evade him. Natalie was his past. But Clementine was his future. He had agreed to reconnect with Natalie for Clem's sake. It had to be done.

Over the hard-slog years of building his fortune, he had learned to trust his intuition. Right now, he had a feeling that Natalie had resisted the idea of spending Christmas Day with him. He'd resisted it too. But now, seeing her, he realised he badly wanted Clem's plan to work.

CHAPTER TWO

A WEEK AFTER her lunch with Clementine in Guildford, Natalie was still no closer to deciding where she would spend Christmas. She'd gone so far as to enquire about a tour of Sri Lanka that still had a single place available. But the more she thought about it, the more she was painfully aware that by running away she would hurt her daughter. And she never, ever wanted to do that. Especially at such a vulnerable time in Clem's life.

This morning she was in her happy place—the airy, south-facing conservatory that looked out onto the bare winter garden, its bleakness broken by the cheerful pansies she had planted. She had claimed the conservatory as her studio after Hugo had died. Now there was only her rattling around by herself in the big suburban house in Guildford. The studio was her favoured place not only for creating art but also for thinking. On her easel was a nearly finished portrait in oils of a black-and-white cocker spaniel that had been commissioned by a neighbour. The spaniel was a sweet little dog, and Natalie was happy with how she'd captured his happy expression. Her client would be pleased.

Her own dog, Freddie, a small, grey-muzzled rescue mongrel of indeterminate heritage and age, lay snoozing in his basket near the heating outlet. She'd decided to foster dogs when the house had seemed so suddenly lonely without Hugo. Freddie was her first and only foster dog. He'd belonged to an old lady who had died, and whose family had dumped him at a shelter. Natalie had found she couldn't bear to send the little old dog back to face an uncertain future. She had become a first-class foster fail.

She put down her paintbrush. She couldn't concentrate on her doggy portrait when her head was filled with thoughts of Jon coming so unexpectedly back into her life. If truth be told, her curiosity about what he might be like now was overcoming her reluctance to meet him.

Her daughter had already formed a warm bond with her birth father. The connection seemed important to her. For Clem's sake Natalie was happy about it, of course she was. Clem had suffered two great losses in the last two years. First her stepfather, who she had dearly loved. Hugo had loved her back unreservedly, as if she were his own. Then Tyler, Clem's best friend, even if they had accidentally made a baby together. Now Clem had found the father who had been, more or less, lost to her for so many years.

Lost to her daughter, Natalie admitted to herself with more than a lacing of guilt, thanks largely to her own machinations that had made it difficult for Jon to claim his visitation rights. She had always painted a good picture of Jon to Clem as she didn't want her daughter to feel she'd been rejected by her birth father. But she knew she could have done more to foster the connection between father and daughter. She had sometimes regretted that as Clem had grown—for in many ways her smart, beautiful daughter was so like Jon and perhaps her daughter had deserved to know that.

How could her mother make things more difficult for her now by sneaking out of the country for Christmas? She wouldn't be going to Sri Lanka or anywhere else. When it boiled down to it, Natalie always put Clem first. She would spend Christmas Day the way her daughter wanted. But she couldn't allow an awkward first meeting between long-estranged former spouses to complicate—possibly ruin—Christmas Day. She had to meet Jon before Christmas—and keep the terms of the 'reunion' in her hands.

Clem had given her Jon's mobile number. She wiped her hands with the cloth she kept nearby, and reached out for her phone from where it sat near a row of half-squeezed tubes of paint. Should she call him? Out of the question. After all this time, that would be too weird. She probably wouldn't be able to find her voice. Instead, she would text.

She typed then deleted, typed then deleted. For Clem's sake, she had to get this right. *Pull yourself together, Natalie.* Eventually she ended up with a message she thought was reasonable. Her thumb hovered over the send arrow, and she realised her hands weren't quite steady. She flexed her fingers, took a deep steadying breath, and pressed 'send'.

Hi Jon, Natalie here. Clementine has told me about the plans for Christmas Day. I think it would be an idea if we met and talked well before that. I look forward to hearing from you.

Immediately she could see someone was reading her text. The reply came quickly.

Excellent idea. I'm free this afternoon. Are you available to meet?

Natalie gasped. In the silence of her studio, broken only by Freddie's breathing, her gasp was audible. She shocked herself with her reaction. The speed of Jon's reply and the immediacy of a plan to meet was unexpected. She'd expected she'd have time to get used to the idea of seeing him again.

Her first reaction was to reply that today wasn't convenient, next week would be better. But wouldn't she then spend that week worrying about the upcoming meeting? She didn't need unnecessary stress. Meet him that afternoon and get it over and done with.

Where to meet? Not at this house. Certainly not at his apartment. A coffee shop or pub might seem too much like a date. She had been planning to take Freddie out for a walk this afternoon. She texted Jon with the address of a favourite riverside park in Guildford, to meet after lunch at 2 p.m. It got dark at 4 p.m. so that limited the time available to see him in case things got difficult. He replied with a smiling emoji, which surprised her. It made her wonder if he was filled with as much trepidation as she was at the prospect of meeting.

Natalie looked down at her hands, flecked with multicoloured smears of paint. The paint would have to be scrubbed off with oil. She felt a rising panic at the thought of what she should wear and that she needed to style her hair. She shouldn't care. It shouldn't matter. But it did. *Jon.* After all this time. She had to remind herself she was meeting him purely for Clem's sake.

Jon was waiting for her in the spot she'd suggested at the edge of the car park near Freddie's favourite walk along the banks of the river Wey. The tall, well-built man was looking the other way, but straight away Natalie knew it was him, even from the back view. Her heart jolted and her breath caught in her throat. She had to take a deep breath to steady herself as she took a moment to observe him before notifying him of her presence.

He was wearing a long black jacket and black jeans that emphasised broad shoulders and long limbs. Back then he'd had the kind of muscles that didn't come from gym workouts but rather from working alongside his bricklayer father on weekends and school holidays. Now he was mega wealthy she wondered what he did to stay fit. She forced back memories she'd never been able to forget of how good he'd looked without clothes.

Did he feel the intensity of her gaze? Slowly, he turned to face her. For a long moment, time seemed to stand still as she looked at him and he looked back at her. There he was—still the same but with changes that twenty years had etched on him. Just as handsome but craggier, more substantial. His hair short-cropped now but still a rich brown, his skin tanned, no doubt from years spent in the Australian sun. He'd been clean-shaven back then, now he sported a close-trimmed beard. It suited him. His face told her he had seen much of life since they had parted.

She couldn't stop looking at him, as if mesmerised, and realised he was searching her face too, with those green eyes so like his daughter's. What changes did he see in her? She'd kept herself in reasonable shape, dressed well, was often taken for younger than her forty-three years.

But why should she care what he thought of her? He had cheated on her and betrayed her at the most vulnerable time of her life. He'd been out there in Australia, thinking he could do what he liked, that no one would know if he got together with another woman. She swallowed hard against a lump of remembered pain. *An image of him with a girl in a red dress still haunted her.*

Her family had told her she was foolish to think their relationship would last—they'd been too young, the odds had been against them. But she'd believed in him. Believed their love would be enough to see their way through whatever challenges faced them. He'd pledged always to stand by her. Until he hadn't.

He took a step closer. There was no offer of a hand to shake, no move to drop a kiss on the cheek in greeting as there might be when two adults without their history met. Just an awkward self-consciousness that seemed to make the air between them heavy and thick.

'Jay Jay,' she finally managed to choke out, scarcely realising what words she'd uttered.

His brows lifted in surprise. He didn't say anything for what seemed like a long time but could only have been seconds. 'Nobody has called me that since…since you last did.'

Jonathan James Grayson. Jay Jay. Her name for the man who had so instantly owned her heart. And subsequently shattered it.

'Sorry,' she said, and immediately regretted the word. She had nothing to apologise for. He certainly didn't seem to be embarrassed at her use of such a highly personal name. A name she had almost forgotten until he was standing right in front of her. He would be Jon to her now, as he was to everyone else.

'No need to apologise,' he said. 'It takes me back.'

'I don't want to be taken back,' she said, forcing her voice to sound steady.

The sound of his voice, deep and manly, had plunged her straight into a whirlpool of memories of the man she had adored. Memories from before everything had gone so wrong. But it had gone wrong. She had been forced to take a path in life she would otherwise never have chosen. Because of him. She had best not forget that.

'Understood,' he said.

An awkward silence fell between them. She had no idea of what to say to break it. She was aware of the slow movement of the river, the quiet splash of a fish emerging from the water, the beating of the wings of a water bird as it took flight, the distant hum of traffic from the A3 motorway.

'I see you brought a guard dog to protect you,' he said. She noticed a slight Australian twang to his voice that certainly hadn't been there twenty years ago.

Natalie looked down at Freddie, sniffing around the undergrowth that lined the pathway. The thought of this little old fellow, who seemed to be a mix of fox terrier, corgi and heaven knew what else, as a ferocious watchdog made her smile.

That was disastrous, because Jon smiled in return. And Jon smiling was devastatingly handsome. His eyes danced with warmth and humour, crinkling at the corners in a disarming way, his mouth curved in an invitation to enjoy life. Her heart thudded into overdrive. How could a man in his forties look so good? Other men she knew of the same age were starting to lose their hair and go grey. This close to Jon she noted a few stray grey hairs at his temples, but they only served to make him look even more attractive. She hadn't got any greys yet. Because she was a redhead, her hairdresser had told her, and redheads lost pigment differently.

'Ferocious guard dog,' she said. 'Yeah. Right. His name is Freddie.'

'He's cute.'

Jon leaned down and offered his hand for Freddie to sniff. He had musician's hands with long, sensitive fingers. Hands that had so skilfully played her body. Now they were calloused. She averted her gaze. *She could not go there.*

'Hi, Freddie.' Freddie gave the tall man the once-over and obviously didn't perceive a threat. Jon scratched him behind the ears. Freddie lapped it up, his tail wagging.

'I remember you always wanted a dog,' Jon said matter-of-factly. 'But we ended up with a baby before we had time to get a dog.'

No way could she revisit those shared memories. She shook her head, pulled down the emotional shutters. 'I don't want to talk about the past. Please. That's water under the bridge.'

'Understood,' he said again.

'I'm only here for Clem's sake. You should know that.'

'Same here,' he said. 'I was glad when you got in touch. It would be difficult if we met as strangers on Christmas Day. Awkward for Clem.'

Freddie tugged on his leash. Natalie started to walk down the pathway and Jon fell into step beside her. She was very aware of, not just how tall he was, but how imposing—the breadth of his shoulders, the length of his stride, how he seemed to take up more than his share of space. Back then, he'd always owned the room. She'd first seen him playing guitar and singing in his husky, deep voice and hadn't been able to take her eyes off him. He'd never been the typical engineering student.

'The purpose of meeting with you is not to have a stroll down memory lane—that's a dead end for me,' she said. 'It's to ensure Clem has the Christmas she wants before the baby comes.'

'I get it,' he said. 'But we can't deny we have a past. Clem's the living proof of that.'

'She is, yes. And I know reconnecting with you is important to her. That's why I'm here, to iron out any awkwardness before we all get together.' She paused. 'Did you have to make the reunion on Christmas Day?' She tried to keep the accusation from her voice but it filtered through.

'I suggested Christmas Eve or Boxing Day as alternatives.'

'You did? I did too.'

'She wouldn't hear of it.'

'Really?' She paused. 'Actually, that shouldn't surprise me. She's always loved the run-up to Christmas, but the most important day for her is still the twenty-fifth of December.'

'She has a point,' he said.

'I agree. I actually saw Christmas stuff in the supermarket in September this year,' she said.

'Premature Christmas in the shops is as bad in Perth.'

She paused. Was this polite chit-chat why she'd called this meeting?

'I… I wouldn't choose to see you if it weren't for Clem,' she said awkwardly. 'But she very much wants to rekindle her relationship with you. That's good for her. She was close to Hugo. She still misses him.'

'She told me what a good stepfather he'd been to her. I'm glad she had him in her life.'

It must have cost Jon a lot to say that. He had loved baby Clementine from the first moment he'd seen her. But circumstances—and, yes, the barriers she'd put up—hadn't made it easy for him to be part of his daughter's life as she grew up. Natalie grudgingly admired the way that he'd never given up on Clem, never missed a payment, sent birthday cards every year. But it had been his choice to live in Australia, so very far away.

'I know you wanted to see her more often. Clem knows that too, and never had any hostility towards you.' *Not like I did.*

'I appreciate that. You did a great job in raising her. She's a wonderful woman.'

Here they were on common ground. 'I'm very proud of her. Not just because she's so clever but because she's fierce in her beliefs, kind and loyal. I enjoy being in her company and believe I would even if she weren't my daughter.'

'She's very impressive.'

'Oh, we had our moments with her. Adolescent angst. Testing of boundaries. Dating dramas. But we all came through.'

Jon was quiet for a moment that seemed to stretch for too long. Belatedly Natalie realised that talking about 'we'—meaning her and Hugo—pointedly excluded him. She hadn't meant to do that.

'Neither of us wants to talk about our pasts,' he said finally. 'But I'd like to catch up on the years I missed with Clem. Are you willing to share more stories about our daughter with me?'

She hesitated for only a moment. 'I guess so. Yes.' He deserved that. So did Clem.

Despite her own feelings when it came to Jon, Natalie had never doubted her former husband's desire to keep Clem as part of his life, no matter how difficult it became. His and her shared past was, however, a no-go zone. She could not, would not, talk about why he had abandoned her and how they'd ended up apart when they'd thought they'd be together for ever. That time in her life had been like a nightmare. She had pushed the hurt way back into the furthermost corners of her mind and never wanted to pull it out to revisit it.

'How did Clem end up with a degree in accounting and cyber security?' Jon asked.

'She was always good with numbers. And she used to tell anyone who asked that she wanted to be a bank teller when she grew up. She loved pretending to be a teller with toy money and credit cards and pretend passbooks.'

'Cute, I can see her doing that. Is there such a thing as bank tellers any more?'

'A vanishing breed, I suspect. Like passbooks. Fortunately for Clem, her dream expanded to wanting to be a banker.'

'She told me she has a new job with an Italian bank based in London.'

'That's right, Artullo's, as a project manager. She's loving it.'

'Her dream job?'

Natalie smiled. 'You could say that.'

'What happens after she has the baby?'

'Maternity leave, but I don't know for how long. Clem has warned me I'll be roped in for baby care.'

'So will I.'

Natalie frowned. 'But you live on the other side of the world.'

'My main residence is in Western Australia, but Clem's probably mentioned I have an apartment in London. I can come and go as I please. The direct flight from Perth to Heathrow takes seventeen hours. If Clem needs me, I'll be here.'

He'd be here? In England? In constant touch with Clem? Treading on the hard-wrought boundaries she had put up between herself and her ex-husband? It would be difficult to put him safely back in his box when he wasn't residing in far-away Australia. Natalie felt too disconcerted to reply. She stopped and let Freddie leave his scent on a tree. She couldn't walk and talk about this at the same time.

'I didn't know that you'd be able to be on call for Clem,' she said finally. *For how long?*

'I suspect you don't know much about me at all, or the life I live now. Like I don't know much about you.'

'True.'

She hadn't wanted to know about him, how his life had progressed without her. She had chosen a life with Hugo and had committed to it.

'What we do know is that we're going to be

grandparents very soon,' he said. 'That means we will be a part of each other's lives for a long time to come.' He paused. 'Like it or not.'

'I... I hadn't thought beyond Christmas Day. But... I guess you're right.' She paused. 'You know I'm thrilled about the baby.'

'Me too.'

'But I'm still getting used to the idea of being a grandmother at forty-three.'

Jon laughed, the same laugh he'd had when he was young, perhaps a little deeper and richer in tone but just as appealing. Even more appealing, if truth be told. 'And me a grandpa at forty-four. But we were young parents.'

So young. And buffeted every which way by their own parents—hers in particular.

'You don't look like a grandpa, if that's any consolation,' she said, unable to stop glancing at how good he looked. He'd be quite the handsomest grandfather ever.

'And you certainly don't look like a grandma.' He paused. 'You still look like the girl I first met all those years ago.' He looked down into her face. 'Just as beautiful.'

She struggled to make her voice sound steady. 'You're being kind.'

'I'm being truthful.'

She fought to keep herself from trembling

as she looked back up into his face—different and yet so achingly familiar. It was a face that had haunted her dreams so many times over the years with safe, kind, utterly unexciting Hugo.

CHAPTER THREE

JON LOOKED DOWN at Natalie, slim and youthful-looking in a dark navy-blue weatherproof jacket, blue jeans and stylish walking shoes. Her hair was still bright in contrast. Did she colour it these days? The shade of red looked exactly the same to him, without a trace of grey.

He wasn't lying or being kind with compliments. To him, it appeared as if time had passed her by. Sure, there were slight creases at the corners of her eyes and the edges of her mouth, and her cheekbones seemed more prominent. Otherwise, her skin was smooth and pale, nourished by the gentle English climate so different from the harshness of Australia. Yet there was something behind her blue eyes that reflected the experience of the twenty odd years since he'd last seen her—not all of which appeared to have been happy. *Was he to blame for that echo of pain?* But she was still extraordinarily lovely—more lovely than ever with maturity.

He had to fight an urge to trace her cheekbones with his fingers, to outline her mouth—just to make sure she was real. Her lips were still as lush and pretty as the day he'd first kissed her. Back then he'd been naïve enough to believe he would never kiss any other woman. And yet he had been falsely accused of infidelity. And the one person who should have been on his side had barracked against him from the other.

He kept his hands firmly fisted in his pockets. After all these years resentment that she had not believed in him still smouldered.

Back then a guy named Andrew, a friend of Natalie's brother, Steven, had told him about the mining job he'd got in Western Australia. Talked up the opportunities and the salary. Jon had applied and been accepted too. Jon had travelled out with Andrew and they'd kept in touch.

It was Andrew who had sent Steven a photo of Jon, taken at one of the rare social gatherings on the remote site, in conversation with one of the drivers—an attractive blonde woman in a red dress. There were very few women in that mining world. Jon had been enjoying the rare female company, but in an entirely platonic way. Not so the woman. Apparently, she'd fancied him and considered him ripe for a fling. The photo captured the moment she'd moved too close to Jon, intent on seduction. What it hadn't captured was Jon stepping back once she'd made her intention clear and walking away from her so fast he'd practically been running.

Jon still wondered what had motivated Andrew to send that photo to Steven, informing him he should know what his brother-in-law was up to in Australia. Natalie's family had immediately assumed the worst. By the time Jon had even had a chance to defend himself he'd been branded a cheater.

Natalie should have been his. Not just back then, but for the time in between. Lucky old Hugo, to have had her as his wife for all those years.

Natalie was wearing gloves, but he could see the shape of her rings on the third finger of her left hand. He wondered what had happened to the wedding ring he had bought her, a narrow band of gold bought from a high-street jeweller—the cheapest one they'd had. He was sad for Natalie's sake that she'd been left a widow, but Jon had had no love for Hugo.

Hugo, the son of wealthy friends of the Lewis family, had made his interest in Natalie quite clear, sniffing around her even when Natalie had been married to Jon. Surprisingly, Natalie's parents had invited him with his parents to Jon and Natalie's small, rushed wedding before the pregnancy started showing, where Hugo had mournfully watched the ceremony.

Nineteen-year-old Jon, arrogant in his youth and confident in Natalie's love, hadn't seen him as a threat. In fact, he and Natalie had secretly laughed about his obvious crush on her. The fact that staid Hugo had been twenty-six to Natalie's then eighteen had seemed, to them, to be somehow obscene. Hugo had been so old and boring. But Hugo had had the approval of Natalie's conservative, snobby parents.

Jon had been shocked, but not altogether surprised, when Natalie had got engaged to Hugo almost as soon as the ink had dried on their divorce documents—the divorce Jon had been coerced into. Her parents had obviously turned their daughter around to their way of thinking—that Jon wasn't good enough for her. It hadn't been easy for him to fly out from the mines in outback Australia in an attempt to stop her from making a mistake, but he'd done it. Only for Natalie to tell him it was too

late; she'd made her choice and it was final.
And that he'd hurt her too much for her to ever
again be able to trust him. Hugo could offer
her everything he couldn't, and she was going
to marry him.

Natalie's parents had never liked Jon, they'd
made that clear from the beginning. Not that
the beginning had been all that auspicious.
He'd first met Mr and Mrs Lewis—he'd always
had to call them that—when he and Natalie had
had to sheepishly tell them she was pregnant.
They had erupted. All his fault, of course. A
boy from 'up north', his father a tradesman,
his mother a shop assistant, he hadn't fitted in
with their plans for their daughter. More to the
point, they hadn't let him into the family circle.
They'd done everything they could to make his
life hell. The mother had been the worst, but
the father had been cruel, too.

Jon had been deemed an irresponsible boy
who had seduced their daughter and led her to
drop out of university. Getting pregnant 'out of
wedlock' was hardly a crime back then, but to
them it had been. How many times had they
told him he had ruined Natalie's life?

Fact was, he'd also had to drop out of university, to the distress of his parents. Student
grants available to the young family wouldn't

cut it—and the room at Natalie's parents' house hadn't come for free. He'd had to go out to work. He had been the first person in his immediate family to go to university and his family had had high hopes for him. They'd blamed Natalie. Although they'd been kinder to her than her parents had been to him, and at least they'd welcomed the baby. He'd more than fulfilled their hopes now, and his father had died five years ago very proud of him.

Now Jon took a step back from Natalie. 'Seriously, no one would believe you were the mother of a grown-up daughter.'

'Must be the miracle face cream I spend a fortune on,' she said, though her voice wasn't as steady as it needed to be to carry off the sort-of joke.

'So now I know something about you that I didn't know before,' he said.

'What is that?' she said warily.

'That you buy expensive face cream, of course,' he teased.

She smiled. He caught his breath at how her smile warmed her face, softening the tension she'd been holding there since they'd met in the car park, obvious in the tight set of her jaw. He thought back to how many years it had been since he'd heard her infectious laughter but couldn't place a time.

There hadn't been much laughter in their final months together. Not while they'd been living under her mother's rule with not enough money to be independent. Not with Natalie having a difficult time getting over Clem's birth. Not while they'd been getting used to having a baby. Their marriage had come under tremendous strain and had begun to fray. Then had come the offer of the very well-paying job in the mines of Western Australia.

But now, like her, he didn't want to poke around in the past. 'Can we talk about our future as grandparents?' he asked.

'I'm sure we'll both do our best for Clem and the baby,' Natalie said a little stiffly.

'While doing our best to avoid each other when I'm in London, you mean?'

'Yes, although I concede there will be times we'll have to spend in each other's company.'

'Understood,' he said coolly.

Her obvious reluctance to have anything to do with him wounded him, her words stabbing through the protective barriers he had formed around his heart over the years. After all, she was the one who had chosen to end their marriage with her accusations of infidelity and desertion. Jon had never cheated on her—not with the girl in the red dress or anyone else. Her family had been only too quick to believe the worst of him. Natalie had leapt on any excuse to be free of him. He'd always believed that. He'd been too young and inexperienced to know what else he could do about it.

'But I think we would handle the situation better if we knew more about each other's lives,' he said. 'It's only two weeks until Christmas. Can we make the effort to get to know each other in that time? Even acknowledge that we could become friends of a sort? You know, bond over our shared care of Clem and her baby?'

'Friends? Do you think so?'

He paused. 'Perhaps not quite friends, although we were friends long ago.'

'We were never just friends,' she said slowly.

An awkward silence fell between them. Was she remembering the fierce passion that had immediately flared between them, the overwhelming obsession they'd had for each other? *First-time love.* He had never forgotten it. Although he'd had serious relationships since, even been married, nothing had ever come anywhere near the intensity of those youthful feelings. No one else had engaged his emotions so deeply. 'You don't know how to love,' his second ex-wife had accused. But he had loved Natalie, deeply and completely. Perhaps there hadn't been any love left in him for anyone else.

'You're right,' he said. 'Perhaps friendship wasn't the correct word. But we are linked through Clem and our future grandchild.'

'Yes,' she said. 'You make a good point. We should get to know each other a bit better. I think—'

There was a rustling in the bushes ahead of them and her little dog suddenly took off, in pursuit of what was most likely a rabbit. The leash jerked Natalie forward.

'Freddie. Leave it! Watch me.'

Freddie skidded to a halt and looked back at Natalie with his dark button eyes. He trotted back to her, somewhat reluctantly, Jon thought.

'Good boy,' Natalie said, as she pulled out a treat from her pocket. She held it out on her hand to Freddie, who demolished it with gusto.

'He's a well-trained dog,' Jon said.

'No thanks to me. He came well trained.'

Jon paused. 'So, there's something I don't know about you that I'd like to know—how you acquired this cute mutt. And what about your flourishing career as a dog portraitist? That came as a surprise to me.'

Natalie leaned down to Freddie to scratch behind his ears so she could avoid looking at Jon while she formulated an answer. Clem must have told him about the dog portraits. She didn't want to reveal too much about herself to her ex, and yet what he said made absolute sense.

Like it or not, Jon was going to be a part of her life because he was her daughter's father, and the baby's grandfather. It would work better if they knew some basic facts about each other's lives. If she could manage to keep thoughts of what he'd been to her all those years ago firmly locked away. Not that she'd ever been very good at that. It had never taken much to bring him suddenly to mind: an expression in Clem's matching green eyes, a way she had of twisting her mouth that was just like her father, a snatch of the song that they had sung together that first night. But she'd got good at pushing those thoughts right to the back of her consciousness. It was the other thoughts of him that had never been as easily suppressed.

She looked back up at Jon. 'Shall we walk on? Freddie is getting bored.'

Jon fell into step beside her, their feet almost immediately finding a common pace. She noticed she was as careful as he was to keep a polite distance. No accidental nudging of shoulders or brushing of arms. But she was intensely aware of his presence. Was that a hint of the same spicy soap he'd used back then?

Jon was the first to speak. 'Clem told me she'd always wanted a dog but that Hugo wouldn't allow one in the house.'

Wouldn't allow. That was Hugo all right.

'That's true. About Hugo, I mean. He was allergic to dogs. Cats too.'

'Fair enough. Although I believe there are breeds that are less allergenic than others.'

'He was allergic to every dog,' she said bluntly.

Hugo had been fastidious. A dog brought mess and chaos, or so he'd said. It didn't matter how much Clem had pleaded, a dog was never going to be allowed. And yet he'd given Clem so much, she'd had the best of everything. Just not a dog or cat.

'So where did Freddie come in?' Jon asked.

'The house felt very empty after Hugo died.'

'I'm sorry.'

'We'd been together for a long time.' She paused. 'Thank you for sending a card.' She wished now that she'd opened it.

'S'right,' he said gruffly. 'I felt bad for you and Clem. Pancreatic cancer, Clem told me.'

'Undiagnosed until it was too late,' she said. 'It was a terrible shock. Sometimes I still can't believe he's gone. He was way too young.'

'It does seem unfair,' Jon said.

She took a deep, steadying breath. 'I really don't want to talk about it.'

Her life had turned completely upside down after Hugo's shock diagnosis. Even two years after his death, she was still finding her place in a suddenly reconfigured world.

They walked in silence before Natalie took up the conversation again. 'I started my dog portraits a few years ago. I'd taken a few painting classes, just for fun. I'd painted off and on over the years but felt I needed lessons. One of the other students loved a portrait I did of a dog. She asked me to paint her Labrador and it went from there. An interest became a business of sorts.'

Hugo had grumbled about her new interest. Not just because of the mess but because, she'd realised, he hadn't liked her attention being diverted from him. But for the first time in their marriage, she'd stood her ground. She'd needed something more outside the office to occupy her after Clem left home for university. Eventually Hugo had agreed to fixing up a disused potting shed for her messy weekend 'hobby'.

'But your subjects weren't allowed in the house?'

'That's right. I had to go and meet the dog in its own surroundings, which was better.' If often inconvenient. 'Also, I sometimes work only from photos. I get orders off my website.'

'Makes sense,' he said.

But Natalie could tell he wasn't totally convinced. Hugo had been everything she'd thought he'd be when she'd eventually given into the pressure to marry him for Clem's sake. He'd been kind, he'd been generous, a 'good provider', but he had also liked having everything his way. It was only after she'd been left on her own that she'd realised how much she'd deferred to him. She would never give up her independence again.

'Anyway, I began to think I would like my own dog. However, I also planned to travel and thought fostering dogs might be a good idea. The idea of fostering is temporary care, to get a dog ready for its forever home, and then hand it on.'

'A worthy idea. So Freddie is waiting for a new home?'

She laughed. 'I fell in love with him and he with me. I had to keep him.'

'Where did he come from?'

'You mean before the shelter?'

Jon nodded.

'He belonged to an old couple who doted on him. They died within weeks of each other. Their adult children didn't want Freddie and surrendered him, knowing full well there was a good chance a dog this age would be euthanised.' She couldn't keep the anger and indignation from her voice.

Jon cursed under his breath, letting her know exactly what he thought of the adult children's behaviour.

'I thought so too,' she said.

'Freddie was lucky to find you,' he said.

'I was lucky to find him,' she said.

'I'm glad it worked out.' He paused. 'What does owning Freddie mean for your plans to travel?'

'I have a reciprocal dog-sitting arrangement with my next-door neighbour. Clem will always take him if I want to go away for longer than a few days.'

'Might not that change after she has her baby?'

She shrugged. 'Perhaps. I'll worry about

that if it happens. She loves Freddie too. What about you? Do you have a dog back in Perth?'

He shook his head. 'Sadly, a dog could never fit into my life. I've had to travel to mining sites all around the world—often in very remote areas.'

Like a child wouldn't have fitted into his life.

'How did you end up working like that?'

Mining had been meant to be a temporary job. Just a year before he would come back to her with enough money so that they could get their own place.

She thought back to that terrible time when Clem was a baby and she and Jon were living with her parents. It had become difficult to stay at Durham once her pregnancy advanced. Her mother had never let her forget how lucky she was that she and her father had taken them in and let her have the baby at their home. She'd suffered badly from morning-noon-and-night sickness, which had made it impossible for her to hold down any job.

For all that, she'd loved Clementine the minute the midwife had placed her on her tummy. But post-partum depression had crept up on her until she'd been deep in the grip of it. Her mother didn't believe in mental illness of any kind—she'd told her to buck up and be grateful for her family support. Natalie had felt as if she were sinking. Neither she nor Jon had had any experience of babies and sometimes simply hadn't known what to do. Lack of money had been a real issue. So had her parents' ongoing hostility towards Jon and his resentment of it.

Looking back, her first months with baby Clementine were a bit of a blur. Because she'd been medicated for the post-partum depression? Or just utterly exhausted, doubting herself, and frightened for the future? She hadn't been herself, that was for sure.

Several times Jon had gone to work for a few weeks with his father in his construction business near Lancaster. His absence had been a relief. The house had been so much more peaceful without her parents picking fault with Jon and him flaring back at them. For him to take up the offer of a stupendously well-paid job in the mines of Western Australia hadn't seemed much more of a stretch from going up to the north of England to work. Neither of them had addressed the issue of their unravelling marriage. She really hadn't been in the right state of mind to be making such a decision. Had he been? Did Jon ever think back to that time and wonder if they could have done it better? Water under the bridge, she reminded herself.

'I started as the lowest of the low, a labourer, when I first went over to Western Australia,' Jon said. 'It was tough. Really tough. Not just the work but the isolation and lack of communication. But I was young, and strong and motivated to make as much money as I could as quickly as I could.'

For her and Clem?

The unspoken words seemed to hang in the air between them. But she had asked him not to talk about their past.

'You became very successful, I know that,' she said.

'I ended up as a mines security specialist, travelling around the world.' He paused. 'But where I really did well was investing early in lithium and other rare earth minerals. Crucial components in modern technology and becoming more so.'

'You invested in the mines themselves?'

'That too. As well as getting involved in minimising their environmental impact—that's important.'

'Clever you,' she said, not sure what else she could say. 'Tell me, did you ever finish your degree?'

'Yes, part-time at the University of Western Australia. You?'

She shook her head. It had always been a regret. 'I wanted to. Thought I'd be able to study part-time once Clem was at school. But by then Hugo's accountancy business had expanded. I ended up managing the practice for the partners. It was a full-time job.' She'd managed to snatch hours here and there for her painting, always wishing she had more time.

But she'd never been able to have any interest of her own outside the family and the business. Hugo had had a way of gently discouraging her. Until she'd insisted on the local painting class.

'Clever you,' Jon said.

'Managing an office wasn't ever what I wanted to do. But I completed some business studies part-time that helped me with my job. I'm quite a dab hand with technology.'

'What about your music? Your singing?'

She shrugged. 'I sang in a church choir for a while. That's all.' Hugo hadn't liked anything that took her away from home. 'What about you?'

'When I was younger, I always took my guitar along with me. Not so much once I got into management.'

She was about to blurt out that they should surprise Clem by singing carols for her on Christmas Day before she decided that would be a very bad idea.

They turned a bend in the path to a stretch of the river a couple of swans favoured. The two floated across the water, graceful and elegant. She always stopped to admire them, and Freddie stopped automatically to wait for her.

'Aren't they exquisite?' she said to Jon.

Swans mated for life. A wave of sadness threatened and she swallowed against a sudden lump in her throat. Back then she and Jon had loved each other so much. *What had gone so wrong for them?*

'We have black swans in Australia,' he said. 'They're slightly smaller but just as beautiful, just as majestic.'

It took her a moment to reply. 'I'd like to see a black swan.' She realised what she'd said and swiftly back-pedalled so he didn't think she was angling for an invitation. 'I mean one day. In a zoo here, perhaps.'

'Perhaps,' he echoed. 'I hope Clem might want to come and visit me in Perth some time. Now she's an adult and can make her own decisions.' He paused and she wondered if he was thinking about her, about them, and all they'd lost. 'Tell me more about your canine portraiture skills.' It was an obvious ploy to change the subject and she welcomed it.

Thankfully her voice sounded near enough to normal to reply. 'I like to paint people, too, although I'm not good enough yet. When I mentioned travelling before, I meant specifically painting classes in the south of France and in Florence.'

She would like to paint him. The more mature features over the youthful face she remembered. He had a compelling face. *That was never going to happen.* She actually didn't think she'd be capable of holding a paintbrush steady, for fear of old feelings it might stir up.

'I guess you didn't get much chance to paint when you were managing an accountancy firm,' he said.

'I've retired from that.' It would have been unendurable to continue without Hugo, although the other partners had asked her to stay on.

'And Hugo didn't encourage your painting?'

'No, he didn't, he—' She stopped herself. She'd had to stage a mild rebellion to get that potting-shed studio happening. 'I don't want to discuss my marriage. Hugo was a good husband and father. I will always be loyal to him.'

'Of course you will,' Jon said.

Hugo had been thoughtful, kind, generous—all those things. He'd also been an uninspiring, unimaginative and plodding lover. Sex had been affectionate but infrequent. Only a rich fantasy life had got her through the years with Hugo—her fantasies always featuring her sexy, imaginative and energetic first husband. She'd been disloyal to Hugo for years in her thoughts. She'd never forgotten Jon. Not when it came to the memories of their sex life.

But she'd never expected to see him again. She felt a blush warming her face and hoped he didn't notice. It would be wise not to see him again. They now knew enough about each other not to stumble around the conversation on Christmas Day. Clem wouldn't care so long as she and Jon showed up. This was too difficult, too heart wrenching.

'We're going to lose the light soon, so we should be heading back. When shall we meet up again?' he said.

Had she agreed to another meeting? 'I…er…'

Jon continued. 'I haven't been back in the UK at Christmas for a long time. How about we continue the getting-to-know-you process by exploring London at Christmas?'

'What do you mean?'

'Lights, festivities, markets, ice skating maybe—you tell me. I'd like to catch up with what I've missed out on by living in a country where Christmas falls in summer. I think you'd be a great guide. Clem tells me you love all the Christmassy stuff.'

How could this be a good idea? 'I do…but…'

Did she really want to say goodbye and not see him again until Christmas Day?

'Day after tomorrow?' he said.

She looked up at him. 'Why not?' she said.

CHAPTER FOUR

TWO DAYS LATER Natalie got off the train from Guildford at Waterloo, one of London's busiest stations. She had arranged to meet Jon at eleven at his apartment on Waterloo Road, refusing his offer to drive to Guildford to pick her up. It would have been pointless and, besides, she wanted to keep the day under her control.

She smiled as she walked by the big Waterloo station clock, under which people famously met. It was all lit up in Christmas colours. A huge Christmas tree, festooned with multiple lights, stood nearby, fenced off from the rush of passengers. London really did Christmas well.

Although she liked living in the suburbs of Guildford, the buzz of London couldn't be matched. She needed to come up to visit more often—which of course she would after Clem brought the baby home to the Kensington house. Kensington was very different from this part of London in that it was so affluent and posh it was home to royalty. Clem was very fortunate to be living there in Audrey's beautiful house. But this diverse Waterloo area in south-east London had a vibrant charm of its own.

It had been a good idea of Jon's to make their getting-to-know-you a Christmas exploration. It was true, she loved everything about the festive season. Also, it would give them something neutral to talk about.

She was still in two minds about the wisdom of spending more time with her ex-husband, but knew—deep down—she could never have refused his invitation. She had to be honest with herself. This—spending time with Jon— wasn't just about Clem.

She had thought of nothing but her former husband since their meeting at the park. Her mind had wrestled with all sorts of what ifs and what might have beens. She wanted to see him, wanted to catch up with what he'd done with his life. Find out how he'd got from a teenager struggling to support his wife and baby, to a man wealthy enough to buy a pied-à-terre in central London that must be worth multiple millions. She knew from Clem that he'd married and divorced again, and she wanted to ask him what had happened to his second marriage. And why he hadn't had another child. All without touching on their shared past. She decided it would be best if she didn't.

She walked briskly away from the station. It was a cold, dull day, but she seemed to get an infusion of energy from being in London—especially at this time of the year where anything that could possibly be decorated was decorated. Was she imagining it or were there even more lights than usual this year? The streets were crowded, but not unbearably so, and she soon reached Jon's building.

She admired the repurposed old factory with the vintage industrial exterior of bare brick and multi-paned windows—very handsome in its own way. She stood outside the large metallic external door for a long moment, before taking a deep breath and pressing the buzzer to Jon's apartment. She noted it was for the fifth floor, the penthouse most likely. Why did that not surprise her?

Jon opened the external door. 'Welcome. You found the place.'

'I did,' she said. 'What a fabulous building.'

'Wait until you see inside.'

He ushered her into the foyer, stark but for an interesting large sculptural piece of machinery mounted on the brick wall, a remnant of the building's manufacturing history. Somehow it looked just right there. Stairs wound away from the back and there was a bank of elevators.

But it wasn't the décor that was engaging her interest. In fact, she scarcely noticed it. It was Jon she couldn't keep her gaze off. He looked so good. How well he wore those extra years. And the beard really suited him. He looked so hot in black trousers, a charcoal-grey cashmere sweater, black boots. A little shiver of appreciation ran through her. This was not Jay Jay, this was Jon. Mature, confident, successful. *Strikingly handsome.* He'd obviously developed a taste for good clothes in the years since she'd last seen him. Maybe he'd always had the taste but just needed the money to indulge it.

Natalie had shown no interest in men since Hugo died. Yet if she saw this man walking down the street, not knowing who he was, her head would swivel.

She realised Jon was taking in how she looked too, and she had to stop herself from self-consciously smoothing her hair into place. She was wearing her warmest wool coat in a shade of deepest violet that reached almost to her ankles, over a lavender knit dress and knee-high suede boots. In the street, she'd stood out in a sea of people wearing winter black and grey brightened only by splashes of colour from scarves and hats.

She herself had worn nothing but black in the months after Hugo had died, until Clem had gently told her he wouldn't have expected her to. She could scarcely admit it to herself, but part of the intense grief that had engulfed her after Hugo's death was guilt. Guilt that she had never loved him the way he had loved her. And the knowledge that perhaps he had been so possessive of her because he had sensed that. She had never wanted to hurt him.

Now, she dropped her gaze at the same time Jon did, and she realised she'd been holding her breath. She let it out on a silent sigh. Of regret? For what had been? Or for what could have been?

Like at the park, neither she nor Jon made a move to socially touch. It did make for a moment's awkwardness, but it was safer to keep a distance. Her mother thought kissing and hugging people in greeting was very un-English. Natalie liked it; she appreciated warmth and spontaneity. But she was glad not to have to touch Jon, even in the most formal and polite manner. She didn't know how she would react. Not with her secret history of fantasising about him.

Maybe she could deal better with his sudden reappearance in her life by putting their past right to the back of her mind. Pretend, perhaps, that he was an incredibly attractive forty-four-year-old stranger she'd just met. But as soon as the thought formed, she realised it could never work. They did have a past. They had a daughter. And, on her side at least, a whole burden of rejection and resentment being booted back into life by his presence.

The lift took them directly to Jon's apartment. Natalie turned around in a circle to admire it. 'Wow,' she said as she took in the vastness of it. The living area was open and spacious with towering ceilings, and architectural details wherever she looked. An open staircase led to the bedrooms on a mezzanine level. The tops of winter-bare trees were visible, swaying in a breeze past the multi-paned windows.

The apartment was all brick walls, timber, exposed pipes, outsized bare light bulbs with bright filaments, metallic finishes in a monochromatic neutral colour scheme. The carefully placed furniture was contemporary and minimalist.

'This place is amazing. Did you commission a designer to do all this?'

'You know how Freddie came to you already trained? This was already like this. I bought new beds and that leather sofa—everything else came with the apartment.'

'Even these wonderful old wooden hat stands?' She picked one up from a display, running her hand over the smooth surface.

'Those too, from when the building was a factory.' He paused. 'As soon as the estate agent showed the place to me, I knew I had to have it.'

She walked over to the window. 'And a view of the Thames as well. I've come through Waterloo station so many times, but I never thought of Waterloo as a place to live. But wow!'

'I like it. It's close to the city, and transport, of course. The Tate Modern is nearby, and the South Bank with theatres and events is only a fifteen-minute walk. You could eat at a different restaurant every day. It's very lively.'

'Borough Market is nearby too, where I'd like to go first today, if that's okay with you.'

'Sounds good to me,' he said. 'I haven't explored it properly.'

'The market is a favourite place of mine,

but particularly wonderful at Christmas with all the specialty seasonal foods on offer. It's a good place to start our tour of festive London.'

Who would have thought he would be walking so companionably with Natalie from his apartment to Borough Market? Jon had wanted to see the open-air artisan food market, now geared up for Christmas, and welcomed her suggestion to visit. It had been a good idea on his part to suggest some Christmas meet-ups. Somehow the very festiveness softened the edges from the inevitable tension between two people so long estranged.

The market, of around one hundred stalls, was on the site of a much older wholesale fruit and vegetable market. Jon had been told various markets had been held on the site, dating back a thousand years. That sense of history was something he'd missed since living for so much of his time in Australia. It was one of the reasons he'd bought the apartment two years ago. He had a home here to return to whenever he wanted. To see whomever he wanted.

The market was decorated with Christmas trees, glittering wreaths and garlands with swathes of fairy lights twinkling all round, right up to the soaring ceilings overhead. As they approached the entrance, Jon was greeted by delicious aromas wafting from the various stalls. 'This place is making me feel hungry,' he said.

'There are always fabulous smells here but more so at Christmas,' said Natalie from where she stood beside him. She closed her eyes and sniffed. 'Roasting chestnuts, gingerbread, mulled wine, mince pies…can I smell mince pies?' She opened her eyes. 'Ah, yes, a stall nearby and with plum puddings as well. And there's the scent of pine from the Christmas trees and wreaths wafting through.'

Her cheeks were flushed with cold, or perhaps enthusiasm, which made her blue eyes shine brighter. She was gorgeous, tall and elegant in that striking purple coat. His charcoal wool overcoat seemed subdued in comparison. All the better to let her shine.

'Are we looking or shopping?' Jon asked.

'Both, I hope. What's the point of coming to a market if we don't buy something?'

'Understood,' he said with a smile. 'What do you intend to buy?'

'Surely it won't be just me shopping. Don't you want to stock up on Christmas goodies for your kitchen?'

He shrugged. 'Not much point. I usually either eat out or order in.'

His refrigerator held only the basics. Breakfast was the only meal he catered for himself. It was different back in Perth where his mansion on the Swan River was managed by a housekeeper. The house was always kept ready for his return from his travels, the fridge and freezer stocked. That the cold efficiency of it all sometimes made him feel lonely, he wouldn't admit to anyone.

'I'm limited to how much I can carry home on the train,' she said. 'I'll see what catches my eye. I don't want to go empty-handed to Clem on Christmas Day. Let's have a look at the puddings on that stall, the one with the little teddy bears wearing Santa hats. I doubt I could make one better.'

'You don't make your own Christmas pudding?'

She laughed. 'I like cooking, but why go to all the fuss that it involves—the weighing of the dried fruit, the soaking, the steaming of the pudding—when I can buy one as good as these?'

'My mother always makes hers in October, steeping it in brandy until Christmas Day,' he said. 'It's like a cannonball.'

'Your mother. Is she…is she still around?'

'Alive and kicking. After my father died five years ago, I flew her out to Perth. She spent six months with me.'

'She didn't want to stay?'

'She loved Perth. But she got homesick and came back to her village.'

'Were you disappointed?'

'She had to live her own life. But it was a good move for her, as a year or so later she met Pete, a widower, and was soon very happily remarried.'

'That's a nice story, I'm glad.' She paused. 'Is she upset you're not spending Christmas Day with her?'

'She knows I'm seeing Clem and is happy for me.'

He could see Natalie's discomfort as she shifted from foot to foot and didn't meet his eyes. 'I'm sorry Clem lost touch with your parents.'

'Inevitable, I suppose. The distance, the—'

'The fact Hugo didn't exactly encourage any relationship with your family.' She paused. 'And I didn't push for it.'

In fact she'd actively made it difficult for Clem's paternal grandparents to keep up the contact.

Jon shrugged. 'Divorce. It splits up more

than a husband and wife.' He paused. 'Mum was upset about Clem, but she understood and accepted it. Now she has step-grandchildren and even step-great-grandchildren to dote on.' And Clem had missed out on a close family contact, thanks to the anger Natalie had held for so long against Jon.

'I'm glad for her,' Natalie said. 'Perhaps... well, it will be up to Clem if she wants to re-connect.'

'Agreed. I have a feeling she might want to—but I won't push it. Now what else do you want to buy here?'

'There's a specialist spice shop I like to visit. Apart from that, let's just look around and see what takes our fancy.'

'Your fancy, you mean.'

She laughed, that lovely peal of laughter that warmed his spirits and made other people turn and smile in her direction. 'You might be right about that.'

CHAPTER FIVE

NATALIE WAS STUNNED at how easily she slipped into a friendly camaraderie with her ex-husband. She'd been so caught up in the fun of Christmas shopping at the market she hadn't thought to be on her guard. He made her laugh more than once. And they enjoyed some friendly back-and-forth banter with some of the stall holders.

She bought her spices, the pudding and mince pies, as well as cute cookies in the shape of Christmas trees, decorated with piped icing ornaments. Jon insisted on buying expensive cheeses and an enormous box of handmade chocolates to take to Clem's, as well as some speciality coffee for himself. They were on their third stall when Natalie realised that people assumed they were a couple. She didn't dare look at Jon, just let the assumptions wash over them. Until she was dithering over which flavours of festive fudge to buy.

'What flavour does your husband prefer?' the stall owner asked.

'My husband?'

The stall owner indicated Jon.

'Oh no, he's not my husband. At least, not any more. I mean—' *Why on earth did she say that?* She felt so mortified she could sink through the floor.

'We're friends,' said Jon quickly. 'Long-time friends. And my favourite is the caramel walnut flavour. But I'll have a medium-size box of the mixed flavours.'

They were out of sight of the fudge stall when Natalie turned to him. 'Sorry about that. I got flustered. I didn't mean to—'

'Nothing to be sorry about. We're a similar age. We're shopping together for Christmas. You're wearing a wedding ring. It's not a big jump to assume we're together.' He paused. 'Friends. Do you think we could be friends?'

'You mean put the past behind us?'

'It was a long time ago.'

'I'm enjoying today,' she said slowly.

'Me too,' he said.

'Can I think about it?' she said.

'Of course,' he said. 'But in the meantime, even though I've sampled everything from chunky chips to paella, I'm starving.'

'We can buy lunch from the street-food stalls or the more upmarket providores. There's an area over there where we can sit at a table and eat what we've bought. But it's very crowded today in the run-up to Christmas.'

'I have a better idea. There's a marvellous restaurant nearby that serves traditional English meals. It's something I don't get much of in Perth and I've been there a few times.'

'How traditional? Like toad-in-the-hole or shepherd's pie?'

'More like a superlative roast beef with Yorkshire pudding.' He paused. 'You didn't used to be vegetarian, if I recall correctly. If you are now, I'm sure they would have other choices too.'

It was a reminder of how little they knew about each other's current lives. And how much she wanted to know more about his. Was he in any way interested in her life or just in terms of how it intersected with Clem's? Did he feel any of the attraction that surged through her when he was close?

'The roast beef sounds good to me,' she said.

The restaurant was all light timbers and glass, white linen and silver service. The Christmas décor was sophisticated and discreet. A welcoming waiter led Natalie and Jon to a circular table for two near a window that looked down to the market below. Natalie was excruciatingly aware that her knees could very easily nudge against Jon's if she wasn't careful. She angled them away from him. She didn't trust herself to touch him, even in the most casual and caress-free manner. Again, the waiter assumed they were husband and wife, but this time Natalie just smiled and didn't deny it. She didn't say anything to Jon after the waiter left them. She'd just wear it.

'This is fabulous.' She indicated their surrounds with a wave of her hand. 'I was expecting a pub.'

'I'm sure the food at the pub downstairs is really good too. I haven't tried it yet. A business associate first brought me here.'

What business? The credit card he'd used at the market had been issued by a private bank that held accounts only for the very wealthy. She noticed how relaxed and confident he was in this expensive restaurant. Clem had said he might actually be a billionaire, if not close to it in terms of wealth.

She smiled at the way he was so gleefully looking forward to his lunch. She had forgotten his appetite for food when they'd been together, especially when he was doing manual labour. She had never forgotten his other appe-tites—and how she'd responded to them. She had to take a sip of iced water to hide her blush at the thought.

They ordered a smoked salmon starter to share, followed by roast beef with all the trim-mings. 'And I'm not sharing that,' Jon said, and she laughed.

'This will be a treat,' she said.

She hadn't cooked a roast since she'd been on her own. She wouldn't bother just for her-self. If Clem was visiting, it was too much for just the two of them. Tyler had enjoyed her meals, particularly her roasts. Before too long she'd be cooking for Tyler's child when he or she (Clem didn't want to know the gender until the birth) visited her. Tyler's parents wanted to take an active role in their grandchild's care too. Of course they'd want to. It must seem like a miracle to have some part of their son living on.

'What do you want to be called by our grandchild?' she asked Jon as they nibbled on smoked salmon.

'That's an out-of-the-blue question,' he said.

'I know. But Grandpa and Grandma seem kind of old for us, don't you think? So do Nanny and Pop.'

'I can't say I've given it any thought. I'm just thrilled about having a grandchild and being part of Clem's life.'

'True,' she said.

'Why don't you wait and see after the baby's born? Clem might have ideas too.' He paused. 'How about Natty instead of nanny?'

'Natty?' She laughed. 'You know, that might not be completely out of the question.'

'I get called Jonno a lot by Australians. But that's not very grandfatherly. I want to be known as a proud grandparent.'

'Because you feel you missed out on recognition as a father?'

He stilled and his jaw tightened. 'Maybe. I don't know. I've always thought of myself as a father—Clem's father—even though she probably thought of Hugo as her father.' He shrugged. 'And to be fair, he did bring her up.' He made the words casual but she could sense the pain behind them.

'Clem told me you were married again for a while but didn't have any other children,' she said. 'Why was that?'

He drummed his fingers on the tablecloth, without replying. She wondered if she realised he was doing it.

She hastily added, 'You don't have to answer if you don't want to.'

After a long moment, he answered. 'I couldn't be a proper father to Clem and I felt bad about that. I didn't think it would be right to have another child. Especially with my erratic lifestyle.'

'I see,' she said slowly, not sure what else she could say. 'Did your wife feel the same?'

Funny, she didn't actually like the words 'your wife' when they were applied to anyone else but her. Which was all kinds of crazy.

'If you don't mind me asking, that is.'

'She said she didn't want kids. Then she changed her mind, but I didn't change mine. But no matter what, it wouldn't have worked. The marriage was a mistake,' he said, tight-lipped.

It was obvious he wasn't going to say anything more. Natalie wished she hadn't asked. She wouldn't dare now ask if he had a girlfriend. Turned out she didn't need to. He brought up the subject himself.

'What about you? You didn't have a child with Hugo.'

'It didn't happen,' she said.

She would have liked another child, for Clem's sake more than her own. But after she'd finally got over the post-partum depression, after she'd stopped the medication, her brain fog had cleared and she'd realised she'd been railroaded into being with Hugo by both him and her parents. She didn't want to give him a child 'of his own'—that would have rounded off too nicely his plans for her life. As a private act of rebellion and—in some way—punishment, she had told him she wasn't ready. She was still young and had many childbearing years ahead of her. As it turned out, when she'd settled into the marriage and agreed to try for a child, Hugo's low sperm count had put paid to his prospects of parenthood. He had refused the intrusive surgeries that might have helped to solve the problem.

'Okay,' said Jon, obviously recognising her reluctance to elaborate further about the child issue. 'It's been some time since Hugo died. Have you met anyone else?'

She shook her head. 'No. I haven't dated. I don't want to. Not yet. Not now. Maybe not ever.'

'Still too soon?'

'Yes. Though I'm not in any rush to get tied down in a relationship again. When you think of it, I never got a chance to be independent. Now's my chance.' And she was loving it. Although there were times she was lonely and found herself talking too much to Freddie.

'I get it.'

'What about you? Do you have a girlfriend?'

'Not at the moment. I don't like to get tied down either.'

'I guess with all your travel that makes sense.'

She wasn't sure what else she could say. Nothing she'd learned about life had prepared her for this situation that Clem's reunion with her father had thrown her into.

Here she sat—to an onlooker it would appear as if she were on a date—chatting politely with her ex-husband, a man who had once meant everything to her. Yet she was like one of those swans on the river, gliding nonchalantly on the surface, paddling furiously below trying to figure out how to handle the undercurrents.

Jon—Jay Jay—was her first lover, the man she had adored and thought she'd be married to for life, the father of her child. The marriage had broken up under extremely painful circumstances. It had sent her hurtling into a relationship with an older man, whom she'd liked rather than loved, for the sake of security for her child. And, to be perfectly honest, for herself.

At that time she'd been in no fit condition to bring Clem up on her own—even with the money Jon had sent regularly every month. Her parents had made it very clear they didn't want her living with them for any longer than was absolutely necessary. She'd had to pull herself up onto her own two feet and stop expecting them to rescue her. Or agree to marry that nice Hugo who was prepared to take on another man's child and would give her a good life. A better life than 'that reprobate Grayson boy' would ever have been able to give her. It was ironic really—while Hugo had made a very good living and left her comfortably off, the 'reprobate' was now extremely wealthy.

Trouble was, she'd loved that Grayson boy, who had made her his with their first ever kiss. While kissing that nice Hugo was pleasant but lacking in passion. She had grown to care deeply for Hugo but she knew, deep in her heart, she had never felt for him what she had felt for Jay Jay. Nowhere near it.

Right now, she had to sit here at this table with Jon and pretend to be impartial, not to feel even the slightest pang at the thought of him with another woman, another *wife*. To rein in her regrets.

She couldn't deny she found the mature

Jon every bit as sexually appealing as she had found him at nineteen and had relived in her fantasies over the years. He was still smoulderingly attractive—more so perhaps. But other feelings she'd thought were long buried had not been extinguished, as she'd thought, but rather suppressed. Spending time with Jon was bringing them bubbling rather too uncomfortably to the surface. She was thoroughly enjoying his company. But could she risk a friendship with him? He was still a stranger in many ways.

Thankfully, before she could think of something meaningful to say, the meal arrived, served with a flourish. It tasted every bit as good as it looked.

'This is the best roast beef I've ever had. Without a doubt,' she said. 'And the Yorkshires are perfect. Thank you for bringing me here.'

'I'm glad you like it,' he said, looking pleased.

They ate in companionable silence. Finally Natalie pushed her plate away—replete, unable to finish her meal. If it had been Hugo opposite her, she would have asked him if he wanted to finish hers.

'Dessert?' Jon asked.

'No, thank you. First, because I couldn't eat another bite, and second, because we want to continue with our Christmas festivities.'

'Where to next? I'm putting myself into your hands.'

She had to clear her throat before she could reply to that tempting invitation.

'First thing after lunch we drop our shopping from the market back at your place. I thought then we could walk around this part of London, crane our necks to look up at the Shard, for instance, which is all lit up for Christmas. The South Bank isn't far and the markets along the riverside walk there are really nice. After that, we could cross the bridge to catch the Christmas market at Trafalgar Square with the big Christmas tree.'

'More shopping?'

'But different. Stocking fillers, handicrafts, decorations, knickknacks. That's the kind of thing they have at Christmas markets. Probably more looking than buying for me, to be honest—and the atmosphere. Except for the churros—you can't miss out on a churro with cinnamon sugar and chocolate sauce. Then, if you're up for it, we can head into Covent Garden and Regent Street. I like the lights there the best and if you're in London, you can't miss them. Oxford Street too, but it gets really crowded. I'm happy to miss Oxford Street.'

'Even more shopping?' he said.

She smiled at the plaintive note in his voice. 'I've done my shopping.' Except for something for Jon. When she was shopping in Guildford, she'd had no idea she would have to buy a present for her ex-husband. But she couldn't be without a gift for him on Christmas Day. That wouldn't be in the Christmas spirit.

'I might need some help in getting a gift for Clem,' he said. 'I brought Argyle pink diamond earrings for her with me from Perth. But I don't know that it's enough.'

'Diamond earrings? I'm sure she'll love them.'

'Well, if you see something extra you think she'd like to have, let me know,' he said.

Natalie thought she could ask the same of him, but she didn't think it appropriate. Yet she could hardly buy him underpants or socks.

'Then I thought, for our next meet-up, I'm giving you a choice,' she said. 'You mentioned ice skating.'

'I haven't skated for years, but I'd like that.'

'There's a choice of ice-skating venues in London. Somerset House ice rink isn't far. Hyde Park has ice skating, fairground-type rides, food, a party atmosphere.'

'You don't sound all that enthusiastic.'

'Don't I? I mean to be. It's wonderful. Hyde Park itself is lovely, as you know.'

'But…?'

'I think it's really more fun for kids.'

'Not so much for grown-ups like us?'

'I'm wondering if you might rather go to Hampton Court Palace. There's an ice rink and the Christmas fair is on this week. It's so beautiful I love to go there any time. Who wouldn't? It's a magnificent Tudor palace, home of Henry the Eighth, and the gardens are beautiful. But at Christmas it's extra special. It's outside London though.'

'Not so far out of London. I last went there on a school excursion many years ago. You've sold me.'

'Day after tomorrow?' she asked.

'Suits me,' he said.

CHAPTER SIX

JON LOOKED DOWN into Natalie's smiling face; it pleased him to see her looking relaxed and happy. Daylight was fading and she was lit by the vertical strings of lights on the giant Trafalgar Square Christmas tree. Other lights illuminated the National Gallery, Nelson's Column and the fountains. More festive lights were strung around the wooden chalets of the Christmas market.

Crowds were milling about, but he and Natalie had found a quieter corner away from the market from where they could observe and listen to the different choirs that were singing carols at the base of the Christmas tree. Natalie had just finished the churros he had bought them from one of the stalls.

'See, I told you these were delicious,' she said.

There was a dusting of cinnamon sugar on her lips. Jon had to fight the urge to gently wipe it off with his thumb. He pummelled down on the thought of how sweet it would be to kiss that sugar off. Natalie was off-limits and to think any differently could be dangerous. If he met her now, he'd be pursuing her, that was for sure. She was gorgeous. But she wasn't a lovely, eligible woman his own age he'd met at a party or on a dating app. *She was his ex-wife.* And she came with all sorts of heavy baggage—on both their sides. He had gone into this time spent together to keep her on side for his relationship with Clem. That was all—and he couldn't risk jeopardising that.

'The churros were indeed delicious,' he said. He paused. 'But you haven't quite finished yours.'

'What do you mean?'

'You have some cinnamon sugar on your lips.'

Her hand flew to her mouth. 'Where? Here?'

'Further to the left.'

'Here?'

'You've missed a bit.'

She wiped her lips with the tip of her tongue, which nearly undid him. 'All gone?'

'All gone,' he said.

'Well, I hate to do tit for tat, but you have a smear of chocolate sauce on your cheek.'

'I do?' he said.

'Only a tiny bit. Lucky it's not stuck in your beard. Wait. Stop.' She reached into her handbag and pulled out a tissue. 'Here. Stay still.' She stood so close he was aware of her scent, a sweet floral. She dabbed at his cheek with the tissue, then stepped back to observe him through narrowed eyes. 'All clean now.'

'Thank you,' he said, bemused by her brisk, impersonal manner. He doubted she had contemplated licking the chocolate off his face—not even for a second.

'I guess I'll have to get used to carrying baby wipes around in my handbag again when Clem's baby is born,' she said.

'So you wiped off my face like you would a grubby child?'

Her eyes widened and she smiled. 'I guess I did.'

'I'm grateful,' he said, smiling back. 'I think.'

How scrupulous they were both being to avoid touching each other. A tissue a barrier between actual skin contact. These two people who had once been so passionate they had made a baby together. Today, they walked beside each other, but as far a distance apart as they could manage, considering the crowded pavements. No accidental nudging of elbows or placing of hands on the other's arm to make a point when chatting. Just friends. Not even friends. More distant than friends. Maybe never to be friends. Natalie had made no response to his suggestion they could salvage something from the long-ago wreck of their marriage.

Her smile widened. 'I'm so enjoying myself, Jon.'

'That's nice to hear,' he said, surprised.

'This was an excellent idea of yours. The celebration of Christmas all around us, it's helped me forget…well, it's been a difficult couple of years. What with Hugo's illness, then his death, the funeral, all of that. It was…terrible. Then Clem's friend Tyler dying so shockingly…you know, the father of her baby.'

'She told me.'

'The funeral was so sad. The parents' grief. Clem's grief. The tragedy of losing a young man with his life still ahead of him. I was very fond of him—you get quite attached to your children's friends.' Her voice hitched. 'Of course, I couldn't help thinking of how unbearable it would be if I lost Clem.'

Jon noticed how she tightly clenched her fists by her sides. He wanted to give her a reassuring hug, but knew it would not be welcome under their unspoken no-touching arrangement. 'And then I've been worried about Clem, having a baby on her own,' she said.

'I'm sorry you were hit with all that at once.'

'Thank you. I like to think I'm resilient but...' She took a deep breath. 'Anyway, I'm not as concerned about Clem as I was when she first told me she was pregnant. She's been managing it very well.' She looked up at him and he could see the remembered pain cloud her eyes. 'So much better than I did.'

'Circumstances were very different back then.' Had she really opened the door, even if only the merest chink, to a conversation about their past? 'For one thing you were so much younger. And Clem has you to help her.'

'And you,' she said.

'Yes. And me.' He took a deep breath. 'The help that you and I can give our daughter will be very different from what your parents gave you.'

Was it wise to mention, even briefly, what they had gone through as a couple? How badly her parents had treated his younger self under the guise of looking out for their daughter's interests? Not when he wasn't sure he could ever forgive her for giving up on them the way she had, of so readily believing the worst of him.

Her mouth twisted. 'That's true,' she said.

'Help from me for my daughter doesn't come with strings or conditions attached.'

'Same goes for any help from me.' He paused. 'Talking of your parents. Tell me, will they be there at Clem's on Christmas Day?'

'No. They live in Marbella now and want to have Christmas there.'

'I see,' he said. *Thank heaven.* He'd been dreading the prospect of seeing those awful people, but would have put up with them for Clem's sake.

'To be honest we don't see much of them at all.'

'That must be a relief,' he said. 'Sorry. I shouldn't have said that. I have no reason to think kindly of them, but they're your parents.'

'Don't apologise. It would be an uncomfortable Christmas with them here. They don't, of course, approve of Clem's situation.'

'Aren't they pleased at the prospect of being great-grandparents?'

'Honestly? I doubt it. I don't think they were ever cut out to be parents, let alone grandparents or great-grandparents. They've never taken much real interest in Clem so consequently she has no great attachment to them.'

'In a way that's sad. In another, I'm glad she hasn't been exposed to their toxicity.'

Natalie nodded, not disagreeing with him.

'As I said before, you've done a wonderful job of bringing her up,' he said. 'You and... and Hugo.'

He had to choke out the words, as he still believed Hugo had stolen his wife and daughter from him. But he had to acknowledge that Hugo had been a good stepfather to Clem.

'Thank you for that.' She paused. 'You might like to know that my parents eventually fell out with Hugo when they realised they couldn't manipulate him as they'd planned.'

He nodded but was saved from having to say anything as the choir of middle-aged people started to sing 'We Wish You a Merry Christmas'.

'Ooh, look,' said Natalie, 'they're wearing sequinned Santa hats. I wonder where they got them from.'

Jon laughed. 'To be honest, I've probably already seen enough market stalls, but I suspect that's where we might find such a thing.'

He stood side by side with her as they listened to the joyously sung carols before Natalie suggested they move on towards the West End. 'We can walk over Waterloo Bridge or hop on a bus.'

'Walk,' he said. 'We'll see more that way. You know, because I grew up in the north of

England, a lot of London is still new to me. I first saw Trafalgar Square and the National Gallery on that same school excursion where I visited Hampton Court Palace.'

'I'm happy to walk too,' she said. 'Sometimes the best part of a city isn't the big tourist attractions but the unexpected slices of life you encounter in the back streets.'

She was right. He enjoyed the markets and the light displays, the shop windows decorated for the season. But it was the unexpected things he was enjoying the most—like an open-top red tourist bus festooned with lights and baubles and a stencil of a jolly Santa in his sleigh. And the courtyard they came upon while taking a wrong turn, decorated not with one large pine tree but myriad small ones in pots, all the same size and garlanded with silver lights and a silver star on top. There was a cute tabby cat with a big red bow around its neck sitting in a shop window that Natalie had to take a photo of. They'd followed the sounds of angelic voices to find the doors to a small, hidden church and sneaked into a back pew to listen to a choir practise for the upcoming Christmas services.

But most of all, he enjoyed being in Natalie's company. She hadn't really changed from that teenage girl he'd fallen instantly in love with. Now she was undoubtedly more mature, a mum who liked to carry baby wipes in her handbag, but her innate warmth and her spontaneity were still there.

His last memories of her hadn't been as happy. He hadn't realised how serious postpartum depression was, especially when Natalie's mother had downplayed it as if it weren't real. All he'd known was that nothing he did seemed to please his beautiful young wife. He never knew what mood he'd find her in, but more and more she had been anxious, tearful, irritable or downright angry. She would slap his hands away if he tried to comfort her. He, in turn, had felt overwhelmed. She hadn't neglected the baby though. They were united in their love and care for precious little Clementine. It was just him who she'd seemed to have an issue with.

The situation living with her controlling parents had hardly been ideal. But when they'd lost their unity as a couple, it had become nothing short of intolerable. The job in Australia had seemed a good idea at the time. And, truth be told, it had felt like an escape, although he hated to admit even to himself that he'd felt a sense of relief sitting on that plane headed to Perth, Australia. In hindsight, though, it had been a very bad idea to leave his wife and daughter—especially in a household that had been so hostile to him.

But now he was with her again. At Christmas. And with his daughter back in his life. He wasn't sure what the future with Natalie might bring. Or what he might want it to bring. But he was going to enjoy this time with her while he could.

Natalie gave herself a mental pat on the back. She was doing very well in her role of Christmas guide to Jon. And a sterling job of hiding how attracted she was to him. But she didn't have to pretend to be enjoying his company. The two of them seemed to find a lot to chat about without straying into the dangerous territory of their shared past.

They'd seen all they wanted to see at Trafalgar Square, marvelled at the beauty of the angel lights on the elegant Georgian curves of Regent Street, and finished up at more shops and a beautiful Christmas tree at Covent Garden. Now they were headed back to Jon's apartment, where Natalie had stashed her shopping after the visit to Borough Market.

She turned to Jon. 'Have you seen enough of the lights?'

'Yes,' he said. 'Like you, Regent Street was my favourite.'

'Enough market stalls?'

'Oh yes,' he said fervently. 'More than enough. In fact, I don't care if I never see another market stall again.'

'I'm warning you there's a Christmas fair at Hampton Court Palace where we're going the day after tomorrow.'

'How about I have a coffee somewhere while you look at the stalls?'

Natalie laughed. 'Actually, I've seen enough too. But well done you for hunting down those sequinned Santa hats.' She'd bought four, one for her, one for Clem, one for Jon and one for Leo.

Would Jon be with them for Christmas next year? She didn't want to ask. Step by step—that was the only way to take this path towards their little family reunion without drama from the past spilling into it and tripping her up.

Jon shifted the bulky parcel he held under his arm. 'Thank you for pointing me in the direction of the wreath for Clem.'

'It's beautiful, isn't it? She and Leo have already got the Kensington house decorated for Christmas, but she told me she didn't have a wreath for the front door. Because it's made of dried foliage and glass baubles, it will last for next year too.'

'So the wreath and the Santa hats will do for next year,' he said. 'I wonder where—?'

'We'll all be next year on Christmas Day?'

He nodded, his green eyes shadowed. 'Yes.'

For a moment Natalie saw Jay Jay again. For all his good looks and magnetism and cleverness, one of the things she'd loved most about him was that he'd been kind. She didn't want to hurt him tonight.

'Are you worried you won't be invited next year?' she said.

He shrugged. 'Clem has her own life. This year might be a one-off thing and—'

'Your daughter is loyal. She has welcomed you back into her life. Christmas is so important to her. If you want to be with her for next Christmas or the Christmas after or the Christmas after that, I can say, hand on heart, that you'll be welcome.'

'And you?'

'I'll be there too.' She hesitated. 'I couldn't not be there at Christmas for my daughter.'

'Did you think about not being here this year because of me?'

How did he guess that? He'd always been

good at reading her. Until she'd seemed to lose herself after Clem was born. 'Well…yes… I did think of being in Sri Lanka for Christmas.'

'Sri Lanka!' He paused. 'Was that really because of me?'

There was no point in lying. 'Yes. I… I was nervous about seeing you.'

'I had qualms about seeing you too,' he said. 'But you've made it easy for me.'

'You too. For me, I mean.' She didn't know what else she could say. 'We've achieved what we set out to do—ease any awkwardness before Christmas Day.'

She was aware of the undercurrent beneath their polite conversation, but she could tell he was no more eager than she was to address those wounds from the past.

'Does that mean that, mission accomplished, you want to skip the trip to Hampton Court Palace the day after tomorrow?' he said.

'No,' she said, too quickly. 'Do you?'

'No. I'd be disappointed if I missed out on the ice skating.'

'Me too,' she said.

Was she disappointed that his disappointment was about the ice skating and not about the pleasure of her company? Probably. But that made it easier in a way. Here she'd been fantasising about him all those years and was clearly still way too attracted to him now, but obviously he wasn't interested in her as anything other than Clem's mum. *As it should be.*

'Do you want to stop for dinner?' Jon said.

She shook her head. 'Thank you, but I can't. I have to get home to Freddie.'

'Is he with your neighbour?'

'He's okay on his own for a day. I took him out for a long walk this morning. He's old and sleeps a lot of the time.'

'Why don't I drive you home? Get you home quicker to Freddie.'

'That's kind but no need. It's only an hour to home on the train, and I parked my car at the station.'

'Sure, but the offer is there.'

'I appreciate it.'

She was happy to go home on the train, but it wasn't just that. She would feel awkward having Jon at the house she'd shared with Hugo for so long. She couldn't have him drive her home and then just straight away turn around and go back to London. She would have to invite him inside for a break. And she really didn't want to do that.

Jon liked that Natalie perched on a bar stool in his kitchen while he sorted through the booty from the shopping excursion to Borough Market that morning. For all his teasing of her, he'd actually bought more than she had.

Much as he loved it, the apartment with its two spacious bedrooms plus an office, soaring ceilings and cavernous open-plan living area was really too big for one person. It sometimes echoed when he was here on his own. Yet it certainly wasn't a family dwelling either. If Clem brought the baby with her to visit, he would have to put some kind of gate on that open staircase. Natalie would know all about that.

'I have an idea,' he said. 'How about anything either of us bought that's destined for Clem's place on Christmas Day stays here? That will save you lugging that stuff home on the train. I can then take it with me on Christmas Day.'

'I hadn't thought of that,' she said. 'But yes, good idea. Make sure the Christmas-tree cookies come with me, though. They'll be nice to serve back home when friends pop in.'

Jon wondered how many friends Natalie had in Guildford. Hugo hadn't struck him as a particularly sociable type, and surely his friends would have been much older than Natalie. He wondered if she'd kept in touch with any friends from their uni days. He hadn't. He slid the cellophane-wrapped package of cookies over the countertop towards her. She carefully put it in her shopping bag.

'This is an awesome kitchen,' she said, looking around. 'Everything so slick and contemporary.'

'Not that it's used much.' He paused as a thought struck him. 'We never had a kitchen of our own.'

'No. We didn't.'

'You lived on campus. I was in a shared house.'

'And then my mother's kitchen, grudgingly shared,' she said.

That had been the impetus for him to take the job in Australia—to fund a place of their own. He still wasn't sure how it had backfired on him so spectacularly.

He turned to put the cheeses he'd bought back in the refrigerator and had his back to her when he spoke. 'What do you tell people about your first marriage? Why it ended?'

He slowly turned to face her, noted the stricken look on her face that she quickly tried to cover with a smile that didn't reach her eyes. 'I tell them we were far too young for it to ever have had a chance of lasting.'

'I say something similar.' He paused. 'Do you believe that, though?'

Slowly she shook her head. There was a long beat of silence before she answered. 'No. I don't. I... I think my feelings back then were so strong that...that things could have worked out quite differently if...if people hadn't interfered.'

Their gazes met for a long moment. 'I think the same,' he finally said.

'But that's not how it worked out, was it?' She got off the stool. 'Now, if you'll excuse me I'll visit your bathroom before I go.'

Jon watched her leave the room, not sure what to think about the conversation. He noticed, as he had in the restaurant when she'd taken off her coat, how fabulous she looked in that knit dress. She'd certainly kept in shape.

When she came back into the room, it was as if nothing had been said. 'I'd best be going if I'm to be on time for my train,' she said.

He got her coat and helped her shrug into it, being careful not to touch her. 'Let me walk you to the station,' he said.

'Thank you for the gentlemanly gesture, but that won't be necessary. Before I go, though, we'd better sort out plans for the day after tomorrow at Hampton Court.'

'Before we look at those plans, I have suggestions for further plans.'

'Further plans?'

'There's so much else nearby here to celebrate Christmas. I remember how much you liked dance. Would you like to see *The Nutcracker* ballet?'

She raised her eyebrows in surprise. 'I love *The Nutcracker.* Yes.'

'And, perhaps, one of the big musicals on in the West End?'

'Yes again. I'd love to. Hugo didn't…didn't care for musicals or ballet. Neither does Clem. I don't get to go as often as I'd like to.' She smiled. 'Another great idea from you. But it might be difficult to get tickets.'

'I've already got them. Ballet for the evening of the day after we go to Hamptom Court, musical the next one after that.'

'How—?'

'I took the chance you'd like to go and procured two tickets for each show. If you'd said no, I would have gone by myself and given your tickets to someone lining up at the box office for standby.'

'I can't say I'm not gobsmacked. Thank you. I'll look forward to that.'

'Wait. Logistics. Instead of going back and forth to Guildford, why don't you stay here?'

She froze. 'Here? With you?'

'I'm not suggesting we share a bedroom.'

She didn't meet his eyes. 'Of course not. I... I didn't think you meant that.'

'You would have your own bedroom and your own bathroom. You could bring Freddie too, if you'd like.'

Expressions he wasn't sure he could identify flitted across her face, except for one that was very clear—panic. Almost immediately, Jon realised he'd jumped the gun. He was at risk of completely stalling the growing friendship. And, deep in his gut, he questioned his motives for wanting her here with him.

'I... I don't think so, Jon. I still don't know you well enough for that. I would feel uncomfortable staying here with you. Even if it would be...just as your guest, I mean a platonic guest.'

'Totally understand,' he said.

'I'm more than used to travelling back and forward from Guildford to London, so it's no hardship for me. Honestly it isn't.'

'Sorry I mentioned it,' he said.

'No problem,' she said. 'Now I really need to be going.'

'Wait,' he said. 'I have another suggestion

for you to consider—and reject out of hand if you think it's a terrible idea.'

She smiled at that. 'Go on,' she said.

'Rather than us going in separate cars to Hampton Court, why don't I pick you up at your place? Then drop you back there after our ice-skating expedition?'

She paused, then shrugged. 'Makes sense. Why not? It's likely to be crowded there and parking could be difficult. I'll text you my address. Call me on approach and I'll be outside on the footpath waiting for you.'

'Sure,' he said.

Didn't she realise he knew her address? He had faithfully sent Clem birthday and Christmas cards there over all those years when he had had little contact with his daughter other than occasional phone calls. Perhaps Natalie was so nervous about spending a night in the same house as him she had forgotten that. He wasn't sure whether that was a good thing or not. 'I'll see you then.'

Now that he and Natalie had broken the ice and started the process it would probably be a good idea to talk to Clem. After all, he wasn't in this alone.

CHAPTER SEVEN

THE NEXT DAY, Jon sat opposite Clem in his daughter's favourite café in The City, the main financial district of London and one of the oldest parts of an ancient city. The area was home to the Bank of England and the Stock Exchange. He was there to have lunch with her. Jon's bank had its headquarters here, as did many others, including Artullo's, the Italian bank where Clem worked as a project manager.

There were, of course, Christmas decorations everywhere there too, but he scarcely noticed them. He only had eyes for his daughter—thankful for any opportunity she granted him to spend time with her. He was very conscious of not crowding her—he suspected their reunion meant a lot more to him than it did to her. She'd grown up with a father she'd loved in Hugo, Jon had only brief, rare times with his daughter up until the age of thirteen, and none after that. But every moment spent with her now was precious to him.

Clem looked slick and professional in a business suit, the jacket of which was cut looser to accommodate her growing bump, although she also seemed a little tired and he hoped she wasn't overdoing things. 'This isn't the poshest of cafés but the coffee is good and so is the food,' she said.

'Looks fine to me,' Jon said. Compared to the food on some of the mining sites he'd worked on, anything served here would seem like a feast in comparison, he suspected.

'I can recommend the pies,' Clem said.

Jon looked at the menu. 'Steak pie. Done.'

'Good choice,' said Clem.

'What can I order for you?' He realised how little he knew of Clem's everyday life, what she ate for lunch even. 'Does your pregnancy affect your food choice?' he asked.

'Does it?' She rolled her eyes. 'You should see the list of foods I have to be careful of, meat and fish not properly cooked, shellfish, some eggs, some soft cheeses, processed meats and so on.' Jon remembered Natalie being as careful when she'd been pregnant with Clem. 'But I don't take any risks. I want my baby to have the best possible start in life. I'll stick with a toasted Cheddar cheese sandwich, please, with the broccoli soup.'

While they were waiting for their lunch to be brought to the table, Clem looked over to her father. 'So, how did it go with Mum? You've seen her twice now, she told me.'

'She's amenable to Christmas lunch,' Jon said. 'You don't have any worries there.'

He decided not to mention that there had been a chance her mother might have escaped to Sri Lanka to avoid the confrontation with him. It made him realise how deeply Natalie's anger with him for the past had run, could even still be festering. And how it could lead to pain for Clem. He could not let that happen.

'That's a relief, I knew she had mixed feelings about it. But how was it for you, seeing her again after all this time? Did you recognise her?'

'Straight away. She hasn't changed much at all.'

'What was she like when she was young?'

'You know she was only eighteen when we met? And I was nineteen?'

'Yes, I do know that. Mainly through warnings to me about not getting serious with any boy until I was older, that it could only end in tears.'

'She said that?'

He was surprised at the shaft of pain that stabbed him at Clem's words. Back then, he had thought he was more than old enough to commit to a lifetime with Natalie. And she'd used to say how lucky she was to have met the love of her life so early. But that was before everything had gone so wrong—so wrong that he had lost this wonderful daughter of his to a man who'd been greedy enough to steal his happiness with Natalie for himself. Looking back, he could see that Hugo had always been waiting on the sidelines ready to pounce and scavenge the ruins of their marriage, even on Jon and Natalie's wedding day.

'Yes, she said that. Along with constant warnings about the careful use of contraception.'

'Really?' he said, not sure he wanted to think about contraception and his daughter—even though she was a grown woman of twenty-four now and very obviously pregnant.

How ignorant he was of everyday dealings that went with a teenage daughter. He suspected he would have been super protective. Again, anger flared at Natalie—and the pompous Hugo—for depriving him of all those years with Clem. Still, he had to hide that anger when he was with Clem. More than anything, he didn't want to scare her out of his life again. He would have to stay on the right side of Natalie to ensure that, having missed out on Clem's young life, he was there as a loving father and grandfather for the rest of it. His second chance with his daughter couldn't be jeopardised by remnant anger at Natalie's betrayal of him.

It still smarted that she had so readily believed he had been unfaithful and then had rushed so precipitously into getting engaged to Hugo—the last man on earth Jon would have imagined would be his successor. No. He had to bite down on any instinct for recrimination and keep things harmonious for the sake of an ongoing relationship with his daughter.

'I hope your mother also told you that although her pregnancy wasn't planned, it was welcomed. You were very much wanted, very much loved.' *And yet he'd let her go.*

Clem nodded. 'Mum has always been very clear about that.'

His daughter smiled and Jon could see a trace of his mother in that smile, of his father in the green eyes that had been passed to him and then to Clem—although the overarching impression was of how like her mother Clem was.

Clem was family—his family as much as

Natalie's—and her baby would be his family too. He would do anything he needed to protect his new relationship with his daughter. If that meant him being civil to Natalie, if that meant never bringing up their troubled past, but rather strolling along on a surface-level, apparently amicable relationship, then so be it. But a nagging inner voice kept pointing out how easy it had been to get along with her yesterday, how very much he had enjoyed her company. How it might be only too easy to be enchanted by her again. *He could not let that happen.*

'You still haven't told me about what Mum was like when she was young,' said Clem.

Jon thought for a moment. Decided to be honest—what was the point of being otherwise? 'She was absolutely gorgeous—heads turned when she walked by. Tall, slim with her glorious hair all the way to her waist, those beautiful blue eyes. I was the envy of the other guys at uni. She was fun, spontaneous, warm, as well as being smart and talented. No wonder I…' He couldn't say it. Didn't even want to *think* it. Couldn't be *that* honest.

'No wonder you…?' prompted Clem.

He thought for a moment, decided after all to continue with the honesty. Clem deserved no less. 'No wonder I... I fell head over heels in love with her practically the moment I saw her.'

Clem's eyes widened. 'Really? Insta love? She never told me that.'

'It's true. And...and thankfully she felt the same about me, though I still really don't know what she saw in me to make her fall so hard.'

'Oh, come on, Dad,' scoffed Clem. 'Look in the mirror. You're still incredibly handsome even for an old...er, older...guy. You're the one turning heads today—women's heads, I mean.'

'Really?' he said.

'Yes,' said Clem emphatically. 'When we were walking to this café.'

He hadn't noticed. Never did notice. Was always surprised when women made the first move. Beautiful women. Smart women. But not one woman had ever attracted him the way Natalie had.

While he was in the mood for being honest, he had to admit to himself that he had never really loved another woman—even the woman he had married some ten years after the split from Natalie. He had been sexually attracted to women, yes. Been friends with them, yes. He had intensely admired other women. But he had never loved them. Not truly loved them the way he had loved his first wife.

He supposed that was another reason he should be angry with Natalie—she had ruined him for any woman who had come after her. But, the truth was, he should direct that anger at himself for being so foolish as to cut himself off from love for so long. Maybe spending more time with Natalie would help lay old ghosts to rest and he could finally move on. Despite what Clem said, he wasn't *that* old. He could even start another family if he wanted to.

'Does this hurt? Talking about you and Mum, I mean.'

He shook his head. 'It's like looking back on people I used to know but have long since forgotten,' he said. So much for his decision to be honest. Looking back to those exhilarating early times hurt like hell.

Clem looked at her watch. 'Okay, so please tell me more about Mum when she was young, while we still have time. They're strict on lunch hours at the bank.'

Jon cleared his throat. 'Did you know we used to perform together when we were at uni, me on guitar, both of us singing?'

Clem's eyes widened. 'She never said. Wow. I wanted to learn guitar, but I was steered towards piano.'

'Piano is good too. Your mum had an amazing singing voice.'

'She used to sing to me when I was a little kid but never much after that.'

'That really is a shame. What about you? Did you inherit her singing voice?'

'We had choir at school, and I wasn't asked to mime the words like some of the others did, so I guess I sang okay. But it wasn't really an interest for me. Besides, Hugo…well, he didn't encourage that kind of thing, or drama or dance. He really didn't like what he used to call "showing off".'

'Seriously, he called performance arts "showing off"?' Jon hadn't thought his opinion of Hugo could sink any lower but it had.

She shrugged. 'That was Hugo, he had his ways, but I loved him.' She paused. 'I'm sorry, do you mind me talking about him when you're my actual father?'

'No. You weren't very old when my marriage to your mother broke up. Besides, from all I hear, Hugo was an amazing father to you when I couldn't be.' It was hard for him to admit that, but he had no choice but to grudgingly acknowledge it as truth. No matter what the circumstances had been, Hugo had brought up Jon's child. And whose fault had that been?

Their lunch then arrived at the table, and he and Clem settled into eating their meal and making appreciative comments about the food. Jon watched Clem carefully as she ate. She still had more than six weeks to go until the baby was born. But even at this relatively late stage of her pregnancy, Natalie had more often than not thrown up her meals. Pregnancy and the aftermath of Clem's birth had been so difficult for Natalie, no wonder she hadn't had another child. But Clem seemed to have a healthy appetite with no onerous side effects pending.

Since his reunion with Clem, Jon had been forced to look into the past. And that had been uncomfortable. The fact he had insisted on staying in Australia, instead of returning home to the UK, had played a large part in his sporadic contact with Clem—especially when Natalie had insisted that Clem would never be allowed to travel to Australia to visit her father. He hadn't had to stay in Australia. He had chosen to. That also had dashed any hope of reconciliation with Natalie. The last-minute trip to try and stop her getting engaged to Hugo had been too little, too late. He'd been inexperienced in life and too proud and too stupid to seek independent advice.

He had gone back to his life in Australia, and

his career in the mining industry, a career noto-
riously incompatible with family life, knowing
that it would put paid to any chance of shared
custody of Clem. Had he talked himself into
believing it would be better for Clem for him
to pretty much stay out of her life? Because
him living in Australia, still at the very beginning of his career, tied to onerous contracts
and barely able to afford the annual visit back
home to see his child, had made it impossible
to nurture much of an ongoing relationship.

The second visitation he'd had with Clem
when she was still young had resulted in his
small daughter screaming at being left alone
with a strange man. She had called out for
Hugo. Jon remembered feeling gutted. He
suspected Natalie, when she'd heard about
it, would have been pleased. She'd have been
happy to have him right out of their lives.

Clem glanced at her watch again. 'Before we
go…' She lowered her voice. 'Mum has never
talked about why you split up. She always just
says it was because you were too young.'

'That's true.'

'But there must have been more to it than
that.'

Jon didn't know what to say. He was extremely wary of treading on Natalie's toes

when it came to her daughter and what she had chosen to tell her. 'It was very difficult.'

'My grandmother says it was because you were a terrible person. But now, getting to know you properly, I don't believe that for one moment.'

Jon stifled a curse. 'Your grandmother would say that.'

'You sound like you don't think much of her.' She paused. 'But don't worry, I don't think much of her either. We rarely see them. All my grandmother seems to do is criticise me, criticise Mum, and my grandfather just shuts up and lets her. I even overheard Mum saying to Hugo once that it was a blessing her parents had moved to Spain.'

'It's true, I don't have time for your grand-parents. I gladly divorced them. But it's really up to your mum to talk to you about…about that time and why our marriage ended. What I will say is that it had a lot to do with fam-ily interference. We were young, naïve, broke and totally clueless about becoming parents, just that we were overjoyed to have you. But the people we should have been able to trust to care for us, and steer us in the right direction, let us down. As I said, it was a difficult time.'

'Okay. I get that,' Clem said. 'But…but I'm

glad we're in contact again. And not just because I'm finding out more about my baby's genetic inheritance.'

Jon reached out and took her hand. 'Me too,' he said, his voice suddenly husky.

Clem kept his hand there. 'Tell me, having seen Mum again would…would you want a second chance with her?'

Jon wasn't sure whether his daughter would think that would be a good thing or a bad thing. He decided, again, to tell the truth. 'No. That would never happen. There was too much pain and anger, and words said that can never be unsaid. I doubt that your mother would say anything different.'

'I had to ask,' said Clem simply.

The waiter came and cleared their plates. Jon paid for the meal. Clem got up to go. 'Just one thing before you go back to work,' Jon said. 'I need a Christmas present for your mum. I believe we'll exchange gifts on Christmas Day and I don't want to arrive empty-handed.'

Clem sighed. 'She's so difficult to buy for. She has everything she wants. Let me think. Not jewellery, she has plenty of that which she rarely wears, and I don't understand why as I love jewellery. She's very particular about perfume and stuff like that. And her painting equipment is a mystery known only to her. But I have an idea. She adopted Freddie, her dog from a local pet rescue. I reckon she would love a donation to them in her name for Christmas.'

'Great idea,' Jon said approvingly. 'And very easy for me.' A very generous donation should make Natalie look good.

'I'll text you the details of the shelter.' Clem got up, a little ponderously considering the size of her bump. 'I've gotta go.'

Jon hugged his daughter goodbye. 'See you next time.' Such mundane words but words that made him feel inordinately happy.

CHAPTER EIGHT

NATALIE APPRECIATED THAT Jon hadn't questioned her when she'd told him she'd meet him outside her house in Guildford. Perhaps he didn't have any desire to see where Clem had lived with Hugo raising her as his daughter. Perhaps he didn't think anything of it at all, except that she might just be a little crazy to be standing out in the cold, stamping her feet, in her down coat and beanie. But she wasn't there for long before he swung into the driveway in his EV sports car.

Jon got out to greet her—again no kissing or hugging or touching of any kind. Jon opened the passenger-side door for her, like the gentleman he had always been, even at nineteen. How her narrow-minded parents had misjudged 'that reprobate Grayson boy'. She faced a thought she'd never liked facing—what had she done to drive him into the arms of the girl in the red dress? Then she immediately stashed that thought back into the recesses of her mind.

It was about a forty-minute drive to Hampton Court Palace, but Natalie had no trouble making small talk with Jon along the way. She hadn't found the right moment to tell Jon she'd thought about his proposition that they should become friends. Now there seemed little point, as it seemed they had slipped by default into a friendship of sorts. She was really enjoying his company. Just like when they were younger, they shared a sense of humour, and even a few tentatively offered opinions on politics. But it was very different now, because they brought more than twenty years of adult experience to the conversation table.

However, Natalie knew she could never be 'just friends' with Jon, although she might give the idea lip service. Not when her attraction to him grew with every minute they spent together. If he had been that hypothetical forty-four-year-old stranger, and she'd spent as much time with him as she'd spent with Jon, she would have kissed him by now—at the very least.

She took her gloves off in the warmth of the heated car. She wondered if Jon would notice she'd also taken off her rings. She hadn't actually liked her engagement ring from Hugo—a large, expensive diamond that trumpeted his possession of her. She'd had no choice in the design. But at that stage she'd been so grateful to Hugo for rescuing her, she wouldn't have dared tell him she hadn't much liked it.

She'd taken off Hugo's rings because she didn't feel comfortable wearing them around Jon. Her marriage to Hugo had always rankled with Jon. He had actually flown from Australia after she got engaged to try and persuade her against it. By then it had been too late for her to back out—even if she'd wanted to. Everyone else had been so happy about it.

Natalie had read Princess Diana's sister told her she couldn't walk away from her wedding to Charles because her picture was already on the tea towels. There had been no tea towels printed with Natalie's image. But there had been a lavish wedding and reception planned by both sets of parents, which had taken a lot of time, effort and money to organise.

She wasn't sure that Hugo's parents had been completely happy about the marriage and Hugo acquiring a stepchild. But as far as his parents were concerned, what Hugo wanted Hugo got. They'd always treated Clem with scrupulous fairness, although their real affection obviously lay with their other grandchildren. Natalie didn't know how they felt about the fact she hadn't given their son a child of his own. When she'd turned thirty-five, they'd given up hinting about when that was likely to happen.

Back then, nothing had been going to stop that wedding and the security it brought with it for Natalie and Clem. She could not forgive Jay Jay for cheating on her. Or for having left her to go to the other side of the world when she'd been so vulnerable. Who in their right mind would have thought it was the right thing to do? Or to agree to it as she had. It had been his fault for wrecking their marriage and Jay Jay wasn't going to stop her from marrying Hugo.

The other reason she took off the rings was that she hoped people would stop taking her and Jon for a married couple. She'd found it a little heartbreaking every time it had happened in London. It reminded her too much of what might have been with her and Jon—and that was a thought that was intruding more often than she felt comfortable with. She ignored the other stray thought—that she had taken off the rings that had bound her to Hugo to signal her independence and single state, not just to Jon but to the world at large.

Natalie caught her breath as she always did

at the sight of Hampton Court Palace, the imposing red-brick Tudor palace said to be Henry the Eighth's favourite. She and Jon had snared a spot in the car park and walked around to the palace.

Jon stood beside her, equally awestruck. 'Isn't it splendid?' she said.

'Magnificent,' he said.

'And the ice rink doesn't look incongruous at all.'

The temporary outdoor ice rink had as its backdrop the glorious, ancient buildings of the palace. The rink had its own kind of drama with the wide expanse of ice, untouched as yet by skaters. It was surrounded by stark, winter-bare trees and twinkling lights strung between the existing old-fashioned lamps. There was a big Christmas tree right in the middle of the ice.

'I love that this royal residence has been here for five hundred years, and we can visit it any time we want,' Natalie said.

'Do you? Visit it, I mean.'

'Yes. I've lived in Surrey all my life. It's easy for me to get to.' She'd been several times since Hugo had died, trying to make sense of the frailty of life in a place where so many had lived and died over the centuries.

'I don't remember it very well as I came here such a long time ago,' Jon said. 'Where we lived, we were more likely to visit Lancaster Castle—which used to be a prison.' He paused. 'No medieval castles in Australia, of course.'

'I should imagine not,' she said. She'd like to ask more about his life in Australia, but this was not the time.

'This castle is so well preserved inside, it's truly like stepping into the past,' she said. 'I've gone through it many times and see something to marvel over every time. As well as the splendid state rooms and bedrooms, I always spend time in the kitchen. It's wonderful the way they have it set up.'

'Shall we skip the market stalls and go through the palace after our skating session?' he said.

'I'd like that,' she said. 'Very much.'

Natalie had booked for the first session on the ice. The lady who fitted her and Jon for their hired skates told them that had been a good idea as the rink would get very busy as the day went on.

As they approached the ice, Natalie got hit by a sudden attack of nerves. 'I haven't done this for years. And I wasn't that good at it even then. I stopped skating once Clem was old enough to go with her friends.'

'I was good as a kid. It's like riding a bike—you don't forget.'

'When was the last time you skated?'

'Two years ago.'

'In Australia? Surely they don't have snow and ice in Australia?'

He laughed. 'There actually are snowfields in the eastern states. You can get from a Sydney beach to the ski slopes in less than a day's drive.'

'Really? That's where you skated?'

'I ski most years in Japan. I have a lodge in Niseko. I've skated near there.'

'There's a lot I don't know about you, isn't there?'

'And we still have time to get to know each other.' He held out his hand. 'If you're still nervous about getting on the ice, let me help you.'

Jon held out his hand to Natalie. She hesitated for a long second, and then she took it. After all these years, Jon was holding hands with Natalie. Her hand fitted as snugly into his as it had that first night they were together. She looked up at him and smiled. Their gazes met for a long moment. She, too, was remembering how wonderful they'd been together, he was sure. Or was that wishful thinking?

'Ready?' he said.

She nodded. 'I think so.'

'Don't worry. I'll catch you if you fall,' he said.

Only back then he hadn't—he had gone away in search of income to fund a better life for them but, deep down, hadn't a part of him been glad to get away? Hadn't it been a relief to leave behind the spats with his wife and the nagging and criticism of his parents-in-law? But, boy, had he missed her once he'd actually spent nights in the mine accommodation, although he would have been too exhausted from the arduous work to give his wife more than a cursory cuddle if by some miracle she'd been there.

Natalie stepped out onto the ice. After a few minor wobbles she picked up the rhythm. Then she was skating alongside him, still holding onto his hand. She smiled up at him. 'You're right, I haven't forgotten.' Her cheeks were flushed and her eyes shone a brilliant blue. His heart ached at how beautiful she was. 'It's such fun.'

When she let go of his hand, he felt bereft. *Be careful.* This whole exercise was about getting to know Natalie in the interests of making Clem happy. Nothing else. Nothing deeper. Absolutely nothing to do with falling for her all over again. That hadn't worked last time, it would be highly unlikely to work again.

Together, they skated leisurely circuits of the rink. 'I think you might want to go faster than I am,' Natalie said as two young men raced past them.

'I'm happy to go at your pace,' he said.

'Really?' she said.

Was she talking about ice skating? Was he?

'I'm here to get to know you, not to be a boy racer,' he said. He had no desire to skate off by himself when he could be shoulder to shoulder with Natalie.

'I'm okay with that,' she said. 'But I think I can pick up my pace. Can you do pirouettes and spins on ice?'

He laughed. 'No. Can you?'

'Sadly not,' she said, laughing.

'When I was a kid, our only interest was going as fast as we could and heaven help anyone who got in our way.'

'I can imagine you were quite the daredevil,' she said.

'Yep,' he said. He liked to think he still was.

He'd certainly taken risks in building his fortune—most of which had paid off.

'Do you know what would make this even more perfect?'

Having you in my life for more than these few days? 'No,' he said. 'But you obviously have thoughts.'

'Snow,' she said. 'Can you imagine how brilliant the palace would look with snowflakes drifting down over it?' She looked upwards. 'Come on, sky, send down some snowflakes, drifting and floating towards us. Jon has come all the way from Australia, and he wants a white Christmas.'

Jon laughed. 'Snow would look pretty but I'm not sure how safe it would be with snow on the ice.'

'So, I'll revise my request and ask for snow to fall after we finish our session.'

'Wiser,' he said, smiling.

At that moment a small child careened out of control and bumped into them. The child quickly gained balance and skated off unharmed, but Jon and Natalie tumbled onto the ice.

'You okay?' Jon asked.

'Think so,' she said a little breathlessly.

He rolled over on his hands and knees, pushed himself up and reached out to Natalie.

'It's okay, I can do it myself.' She was quickly back on her feet.

Jon pulled her into his arms for a hug. 'Are you sure you're all right?'

'That wasn't the first fall on ice I've had,' she said, though her voice still sounded a little shaky.

It had been so long since he had held her close. She fitted perfectly against him—as well, that was, as two puffer jackets allowed. He tightened his arms around her. Natalie seemed in no rush to release herself from his hug, but he didn't want to take things in this direction. Still, it was with reluctance he released her.

'Our skating session is coming to an end,' he said. 'How about we do one more circuit, then find a hot chocolate before we tour the castle?'

'And then I'll need you to take me home,' she said. 'I need to put the finishing touches to my cocker spaniel portrait. I promised the owner I'd have it ready for Christmas. She wants to give it to her husband as a present. You won't mind if I don't ask you in, will you?'

Jon hadn't expected to be invited in. In fact he never wanted to be inside the home Natalie had shared with Hugo. And yet he'd hoped to extend the day a little longer as he so enjoyed their time together he knew he'd miss her when he said goodbye. And he hadn't expected that. He was careful to keep a friend-zone distance between them as they explored the palace.

CHAPTER NINE

NATALIE HADN'T BEEN completely honest with Jon. Yes, it was true she had to work on the cocker spaniel portrait, although she'd nearly completed it the day before. Now it was only a matter of adding a few highlights and it would be done.

But the real reason she needed to get home early was that Clem was coming for dinner, taking the train down from London after work. It was actually a portrait of her pregnant daughter she wanted to work on. Natalie didn't feel she needed to explain that to Jon—nor did she want to invite him to share the meal with them. Christmas Day would be time enough for the three of them to be together. Tonight she wanted her darling daughter to herself.

She'd made one of Clem's favourite meals, an Italian-style chicken casserole with red onion and tomatoes, rich with thyme and garlic. She'd serve it with noodles and broccoli, again favourites of Clem's. It wasn't often these days she got to treat her daughter.

Natalie left the casserole in the oven when she went to pick Clem up from the station. As soon as she came into the house, Clem sniffed appreciatively at the aroma wafting from the kitchen. 'Aah, you've cooked The Chicken. Thanks, Mum. Just what I feel like on a chilly night like this.' That was what Clem always called the dish, as if it were the only way chicken could ever be cooked.

Natalie helped Clem off with her coat. She stood back from Clem to admire her. 'Just look at that bump. It's absolutely beautiful. But you seem a little weary, sweet pea. Are you sleeping?'

'Seems to get bigger every day,' said Clem. 'And it can be tiring carting it around.'

'If you're like me, your bump will get so much bigger as you get closer to your due date. You've still got more than six weeks to go. I was enormous with you. We've got tall people in our family and Tyler was tall, too. Can you feel the baby kicking?'

'I think he or she will be a footballer. I can actually see a little foot rippling my tummy sometimes as it kicks, which is fun.'

'Such fun, sweet pea,' Natalie said, at the

same time thinking it was sad Tyler wasn't there to share in the excitement of their developing baby's milestones. As she and Jon had. More and more she found herself remembering some of the good times they'd shared that had been eclipsed by the awful ones that had followed. 'I can't wait to meet my little grandbaby. But try and rest more. When do you knock off work to go on maternity leave?'

'Theoretically, it could be as early as now. But I want to work as long as I can. I have so much to do, and I'd be bored being at home just waiting, so I'm going at the end of December.'

'You might be glad of a break when that time comes. You'll want to nest.'

She and Clem sat down for dinner at the kitchen table. She hadn't used the dining room since Hugo had got ill. Freddie sat by Clem's feet hoping for snacks. Natalie turned a blind eye to the pieces of chicken Clem surreptitiously fed to the little dog.

'Mum, I worry about you all by yourself in this big house.'

'Don't be,' Natalie said. 'I have Freddie for company, remember.'

Clem laughed. 'Hugo would have been horrified if he'd known you'd have a dog sleeping on your bed.'

'I know,' Natalie said, smiling. After the grief of Hugo's loss, it was nice Clem could talk about him so naturally.

'Do you think you're ready to date yet?' Clem asked, out of the blue.

'No. I'm not sure I ever will be. I'm enjoying my independence too much to give it up for a man.'

'You could just have affairs.'

'Clem!'

'C'mon, Mum, you're still very attractive, you know. Some of my guy friends at uni used to call you a MILF.'

'What's that? A compliment or an insult?'

'Actually it means a Mum I'd Like to F—'

'Clem! Stop right there. I'm horrified.'

'And just the teeniest bit chuffed?'

'No! I'm not interested in compliments from horny adolescent boys.'

'Although you married one first time round. Dad tells me you were absolutely stunning when you were eighteen. I reckon he must have been stunning too when he was nineteen.'

'He was. He was so good-looking. And charming with it.'

'He's still handsome.'

Natalie put down her fork. 'Wait. You were talking about me with Jon?'

'I had a quick lunch with him yesterday.'

'What did he say?'

'That you were head over heels in love with each other.'

She didn't want to admit any such thing to her daughter but her thoughts sent her back to the past. She sighed. 'We were. We were absolutely smitten.'

'What went wrong?'

'Did you ask Jon that?' Natalie said cautiously.

'I did. But he wouldn't say much more than you were too young and it was a difficult time.'

'That was the truth,' Natalie said firmly.

'But if you were that much in love, why didn't you make it work?'

'I don't know.' Natalie had to be careful about what she said to Clem. 'Circumstances were different. We had to live with my parents, for one thing.'

Clem groaned. 'That must have been hell.'

'It was. But I can't blame them for everything. Jon and I were at fault too.'

He cheated on me—with a girl in a red dress. It all came down to that. Other problems might have been solved. But not once she'd known about that. Of course she would never say that to Clem. She didn't want her daughter to think badly of her birth father. He had tried his best to be an absentee father and she had thwarted him all the way—a fact she now felt bad about. He had always given financial support, even in those early years when it must have been a stretch.

Now, as she saw how much Clem liked him, Natalie's guilt over her role in keeping them apart intensified. But it had seemed the right thing to do at the time. Clem had needed a stable father figure, and Hugo had been that and more. There had been no room for Jon in their lives.

'But at least you've had that passionate, all-encompassing love, that mad attraction. I... I never had it with Tyler...' Clem's voice trailed away.

'I know, sweet pea, I really do.'

Clem's mouth turned downward. 'I just hope...someone can really be okay with taking on another man's child.'

'What? Do you mean Leo? Has he said anything about that?'

Clem's face clamped down. Natalie knew that evasive look. 'I... I was talking hypothetically.'

Natalie frowned. 'Are you sure about that?'

'Very sure.' Clem paused. 'I know you didn't have it with Hugo.'

'What do you mean?'

'That mad, passionate attraction. You loved Hugo, I know that. And you know I adored him. But you weren't ever *in love* with him.'

'Whatever would make you say that?'

'Observation,' said Clem smugly.

'Well, you were wrong,' said Natalie, knowing she was lying.

'No, I wasn't. But I'm not judging. Love is love. Sometimes you have to take what you can get and that's good enough.'

When did her little girl get so thoughtful? And had she noticed the cracks in her marriage to Hugo? Natalie had thought she'd done a good job in plastering them over.

Clem continued. 'But I do wonder why you let the real deal go with Dad. And I'm wondering if you could get it back together with him.'

'Clem! What's got into you tonight? Of course I'm not going to get back with Jon. After all these years.' Not with a man who'd hurt her so badly.

'You've already spent two days out with him. How did they go?'

Natalie pushed her plate away and got up from the table. 'If you must know, they went really well. We got on famously. I like him. But we're only spending time together to get to know each other again for your sake. It will be easier for you if your baby's grandparents aren't at loggerheads.'

'You're sure about that? That's the only reason?'

'Yes.' She took a deep breath, walked from the table and back to face Clem. 'The thing is, when you have a love like we had back then it really hurts when it crashes and burns. It leaves wounds—wounds that never really heal. I have no intention of picking at the scars that have grown over those wounds.'

'Sorry, Mum, I didn't realise.'

Natalie put her hands on Clem's shoulders. 'Of course you didn't, sweet pea. It might seem all romantic hearts and flowers that two people who'd felt so strongly about each other when they were young, who'd had the most amazing child, might fall back into each other's arms when they meet again twenty years later—one widowed, the other divorced. But that's pure fantasy. It's not going to happen. There's a literal ocean between me in England and Jon in Australia. But there's also an ocean of pain and loss. All is not going to be forgiven. It's way too late for that.'

'I… I didn't realise, I'm so sorry, Mum,' Clem said again.

Natalie sat down in her chair toface Clem. 'Don't be sorry, sweet pea. Because I think Jon and I might be able to salvage a friendship of sorts, united by our love for you and our joy in our grandbaby.'

'Seriously?'

'Yes.'

'Are you going to see him again before Christmas Day?'

'Guess what? He's booked tickets for *The Nutcracker* for tomorrow night and that hot new musical for the night after.'

'Really? That's amazing. For one thing I've heard it's impossible to get tickets to the musical.'

'He got them.'

'A very fat wallet can work wonders, I believe.'

Natalie laughed. 'Perhaps.'

'And another thing, I'm thrilled that he's willing to go with you. Not like me and Hugo having to be dragged along, unwilling and protesting.'

Natalie laughed. 'True.'

Clem smiled. 'I'm glad you're going to be friends with Dad. You're right. It will make it easier for you to be co-grandparents. One day, perhaps, you'll each have new partners and it will all be very civilised.'

Jon with a new partner? Natalie wasn't sure that she liked that idea at all. She would find it difficult to see him with another woman. She never had. Just that girl in the red dress in the photo that had done so much to destroy their marriage. And the wounds from that still throbbed.

She forced her voice to sound normal. 'Yes. That would indeed be civilised.'

'You'll be doing a lot of to-ing and fro-ing from London going to the theatre two nights in a row.'

'Actually, Jon suggested I stay at his apartment. He has a guest bedroom.'

'That's a good idea.'

'Of course, I said no.'

'Why? It's an awesome place and you could walk to everything.'

'I… I wouldn't feel comfortable about it.'

'Why is that? I think you'd be safe with Dad. You're just friends, right?'

'Yes, but I—'

Clem got up from her chair. 'I'd feel a lot happier if you stayed at Dad's. Safer than coming home on a late train to a creepy car park and then an empty house.'

'So now you're looking after me, darling daughter.'

'Hugo always did. I told you, I worry about you being alone in this house.'

'I'm really okay on my own, sweet pea. But I love your concern for me.'

Clem gave her a somewhat cumbersome hug, her bump getting in the way. 'Always, Mum, always.'

'Thank you. That means a lot.'

'So you'll stay at Dad's?'

'What about Freddie?'

'You know your neighbour will take him.'

'You're right. I'll text Jon to see if the offer is still open,' Natalie said.

'I'm sure it will be,' said Clem.

'Now, before I drive you home to Kensing-ton—'

'No need to do that. I—'

Natalie put up her hand to ward off Clem's protest. 'Driving you home is not negotiable.'

'You really don't have to, Mum.'

'But I want to, right?'

'Right. You win.'

'Before you go, I'd like you to pop into my studio and sit for me for just ten minutes.'

'For my pregnant portrait?'

'Yes. It's nearly done but seeing you tonight makes me want to make that lovely bump of yours a little more prominent. I think this is the perfect moment of your journey to motherhood to capture in oils. I'm really pleased with how the portrait is coming along and I think you will be too.'

'Then you'll text Dad to confirm you'll stay in his apartment?'

'I promise I'll do that,' Natalie said.

CHAPTER TEN

THE PREVIOUS NIGHT, Natalie had won the battle to drop her pregnant daughter safely back home to the Kensington town house. But she'd lost the battle with Jon when he wanted to drive down and pick her up from Guildford and take her back to his apartment.

He had totally overridden her protests. 'I'm just being practical,' he'd said. 'So you drive yourself to Waterloo in your car and get slammed by exorbitant London parking charges, not to mention congestion charges. You take the train, and you'll have to leave your car in the station car park for several days. Just let me pick you up. I enjoy the drive.'

Natalie had agreed without too much protest. It was nice to be driven and what Jon had said made sense.

Jon picked her up early the following afternoon. He took her overnight bag and stashed it in his boot. She handed him a large stiff folder tucked into a padded shopping bag.

His brow furrowed. 'What's this?'

'I'll show you later,' she said with a smile. 'Please make sure it doesn't get squashed.'

He carefully placed the folder in the boot alongside her case. 'I'm curious. It doesn't seem like something to eat.'

'It's definitely not edible.'

'Then what—?'

'You'll have to wait and see.'

The contents of that folder were far too precious to be playing guessing games over. She'd show it to him later, when they were back at his apartment.

On the way to Waterloo, they chatted about what they'd seen at the palace the day before and about Clem's decision to stay on at work for a few more weeks. As they spoke, Natalie realised how much Jon cared for his daughter and she sank into her guilt about her active role in keeping him from Clem. It had been a tit-for-tat situation when she'd still been consumed by anger and grief and post-partum depression—you cheat on me and break my heart, I keep you from your daughter. She wouldn't be that mean now, after realising that a child couldn't be too loved.

She was so lost in her thoughts, she only realised Jon had driven into an underground car park as they were heading down a ramp.

'I rent a secure car space here. My apartment block is just around the corner,' he explained.

Natalie could only imagine what that car space would cost in central London. Jon told her he kept his car there, so it would be ready any time he decided to come to London. 'Perhaps Clem could use the car sometimes if she needs it,' he said.

'That's very kind of you.'

'She's my daughter,' he said, as if that were explanation enough for his generosity which, she supposed, it was.

Once they were in Jon's apartment, Natalie followed Jon up the open staircase that led to the mezzanine level and into his guest room. Like the rest of his apartment, it was worthy of a feature in a high-end interiors magazine, minimalist yet obviously designed for comfort. There was also a beautifully appointed en suite bathroom, complete with steam shower. Jon put her overnight bag on the floor next to the bed.

'Show me where the sheets are, and I can make up the bed,' she said.

'Already done,' he said. 'I called in the team from the housekeeping service company I use.

They came this morning. Your bed is made, there are fresh towels in the bathroom, toiletries have been refreshed. The fridge has been stocked with a few essentials.'

'Like a hotel,' Natalie said, bemused at his efficiency.

This was a far cry from his shoebox-sized bedroom in the shared student house in Durham where they'd had to put a chair up against the door to ensure privacy.

She followed him back down the stairs. If Clem ever brought the baby here, Jon would have to fit stair gates, that was for sure.

'Do you want your folder in your room too?'

She shook her head. 'I'll keep it with me,' she said.

'Still not a hint as to what's in there?' he teased.

'Not a one,' she responded with a smile. 'Shall we have tea?'

'There are various teas in the pantry, choose whichever you like.'

Natalie made the tea and took it over to the coffee table. She put some of the Christmas shortbread Jon had bought at Borough Market on a plate and took that too.

They sat side by side on the leather sofa and had their tea in companionable silence. After she had finished her cup of tea, Natalie got up to retrieve the folder from where she'd left it on the dining table and brought it over to where Jon sat.

'The secret is about to be revealed at last?' he said, raising a curious eyebrow.

'Yes,' she said. 'I want to talk to you about this.' She took the folder from the shopping bag that had protected it. 'I'm sure Clem mentioned that we will exchange gifts on Christmas Day at her place.'

'She did.'

'Of course I want to have a gift for you.'

He protested. 'You don't need to—'

'I do,' she said firmly. 'I didn't see anything I thought you'd like while we were out shopping. Then I had an idea.' She patted the seat of the sofa. 'Here, sit closer to me so I can show you. If you like this gift, I'll wrap it to give it to you on Christmas Day.'

'I'm really curious now,' he said as he scooted closer to her on the sofa.

Natalie placed the folder on her lap where he could easily see it. She lifted out a pile of paintings on heavy quality cartridge paper, separated by sheets of tissue paper. She lifted up the first to show him—a watercolour of a delightfully chubby baby with a wisp of auburn hair, looking up out of the picture with wide green eyes and a sweet baby smile.

'It's Clem,' said Jon, peering closely at it. 'It's baby Clementine. Wow. Did you paint this?'

'Yes.'

He continued to stare at the painting in awe. Natalie found she was twisting her hands together, in anticipation of his reaction.

Finally he took his eyes off the painting. 'It's incredible. Such a likeness. And her personality shines through. How old is she here?'

'Six months. I did it after you left for Australia and when I was still living with my parents. Do you like it?'

'I love it.' He slowly shook his head. 'You're so talented. I can't believe how you've captured the likeness.'

Natalie couldn't help but be pleased at his reaction. 'There are more.' She indicated the stack of other paintings beneath. 'Since then, I've done so many paintings and sketches of our daughter at different ages, right up until now. I'm working on an oil of her pregnant, with her hands on her belly. She's dreamy as she looks both inward and forward to when she meets her baby.'

'That would be beautiful,' he said, his voice husky. 'I'd like to see it when it's finished.'

'I was learning and, I hope, improving, so did multiple attempts at capturing the same poses. Not that Clem had the patience to stay still and pose for long. I took photos as well to work with. I was a stay-at-home mum for Clem's first years, that's when I started.'

'Can I see the others?' he said, indicating the stack.

'Of course. You asked me to fill you in on more stories of Clem. I went through and picked out some of my favourites that I've done. There are ten paintings here, mainly watercolours. They're slightly different from the ones I've kept.'

'For me? These are for me? To keep?'

'You might want to look at them first, before you say you want to keep them. Go on, unwrap them from the tissue paper.'

She'd stacked the paintings in chronological order. Jon exclaimed over paintings of adorable toddler Clem, through to seven-year-old Clem grinning with no front teeth and freckles scattered over her nose, and then to teenage Clem with her stance slightly rebellious, graduate Clem in her university gown laughing and tossing her mortar board in the air, and finally to

Clem hugging Freddie, ecstatic to have a dog in the family at last.

'These are…incredible, perfect, priceless,' he exclaimed. 'You have such a gift. Are you sure you want to give them to me?'

'I have so many others. Believe me. And who better to give them to than you, her other parent?'

'I don't know what to say. Except thank you.'

'So, this is an acceptable present to give you on Christmas Day?'

'I couldn't think of anything I'd like more,' he said frankly.

A little of her guilt felt assuaged by his reaction. Not that a series of paintings could make up for all those missed visits to a real-life daughter. But he'd chosen to stay in Australia, so the estrangement from his daughter wasn't all on Natalie.

'I'll buy a rigid artist portfolio to transport them, as you'll be travelling home to Australia with them.'

When would he be going? Straight after Christmas? The thought of not being able to see him was unbearable.

'I hope my gift helps make up for those years you missed out on with Clem,' she said.

'Nothing can make up for those lost years,'

he said, his eyes sad. 'But this will help in some way.'

'I'm glad,' she said, choking up.

Jon turned to her directly. He searched her face for what seemed an age but must only have been seconds. She could see the shadows of over twenty years of pain in his eyes. 'Nothing can ever make up for all the years I lost with you, either.'

Her heart started to hammer so fast he surely must hear it. Her mouth went dry and she couldn't have stuttered out an answer even if she wanted to. Because she couldn't think of a word to say in reply.

Finally, she managed. 'I know.'

'Do you ever wonder how it unravelled so quickly for us?' he said. 'Why we didn't fight harder for what we had? Because what we had was special—I've never found it again. Do you ever think about it?'

Her voice came out as a whisper, broken and uneven. 'I've thought of nothing else since we've been seeing each other.'

Natalie turned her head away but Jon reached out with a hand on her cheek and gently turned her around so she again faced him. She reached up and placed her hand over his on her cheek. For a very long moment they looked into each other's eyes. *Jon, not Jay Jay.* She took a deep breath and let it out on a sigh of surrender. She couldn't fight her attraction to him any longer.

She reached out for him at the same time he reached for her, so they were seamlessly wrapped in each other's arms. She shifted in her seat to press closer to him, closed her eyes to better savour the sensation of his body next to hers. He was still the same but more muscular, more powerful. She breathed in the scent of him, that same spicy soap he'd used so long ago that unleashed a stream of memories. The thought ran persistently through her mind: *Back where I belong.*

His lips met hers in a kiss, tentative, questioning and she kissed him back. *At last.* She relaxed against him and he deepened the kiss. She had imagined this kiss in her fantasies, but the reality was so much more exciting—tender yet arousing, releasing a joy that had been denied to her for so long. The way he kissed her was so familiar, and yet something was very different. His beard, that was what it was. Back then he'd been clean-shaven. The soft brush of his beard on her skin was a new sensation. She liked it. This was where she wanted to be.

Their kiss grew deeper. She felt desire stirring, making demands, *wanting him.* She had loved Jay Jay so much, she almost believed she could feel the same for Jon. Never dreamed she'd have a second chance with him, after all those years without him. She felt flooded by emotions so deep and conflicting she was overwhelmed by the urge to cry. She broke away from the kiss as she fought the tears, but her body shook with sobs. She shoved him away from her.

'What's wrong?' he asked, bewildered.

She got up from the sofa. Walked a few steps away. Turned back to face him. 'You are.'

Jon jumped up from the sofa. 'What do you mean? Why are you crying?'

'For everything we lost,' she choked out.

She gave into the tears, let them flow from her eyes and slide down her cheeks as she faced him. The words poured out. 'We were so good together. What we shared was beautiful. Why did you throw it away? You were my first lover, my only lover. Making love with you was so special. Your body was mine and mine was yours. It was like a…a desecration that you had sex with that girl in the red dress. It was agony for me to think about you giving her what was mine.'

Jon stepped closer. He bumped the edge of the coffee table and a teacup fell, smashing on the hard wooden floor. Natalie gasped. He ignored it, just stepped around the shards of broken china.

'But I didn't have sex with her, Natalie. Not for want of trying on her part, I admit, but I wasn't interested. Why would I want her when I had the most wonderful woman in the world as my wife?'

'I wasn't there to be a wife to you. There was a photo of you together—she was all over you.'

Anger rumbled through Jon's voice. 'She came after me the night that photo was taken. She was drunk. It was embarrassing. I told her I wasn't interested. I was married. I walked away from her.'

'But my brother Steven's friend, Andrew, told him everyone on that site knew you were with her.'

'Hearsay. It wasn't true. Where was the proof?'

'Steven said Andrew's word was proof, as was the photo. Why would he lie?'

Jon cursed fiercely. 'I don't know. But he did lie. Unless…he either wanted you for himself—maybe he had a crush on his friend's little sister—or he'd wanted that Australian girl and was jealous.'

The incident had happened so long ago, but

Natalie remembered it only too well. But could Andrew have had a hidden agenda? She'd certainly never had any interest in him. And it was he who had enticed Jon to go to Australia with promises of big money.

'That's not what Andrew told Steven. He said life back home was forgotten out on those remote mining sites. Morals and loyalties went out of the window and into the red dust. He said that people worked incredibly long hours because there was nothing else to do, and the men went feral when they had time off. Men way outnumbered women and the women could have their pick of the men.' She paused. 'The look on the face of that girl in the photo was feral. She was hungry for you.'

'Well, I didn't want her.' He paused. 'Some of what you said about life out there was true. It could be rough.'

Natalie gasped.

'Except that I never had anything to do with that girl,' he said harshly. 'I never even touched her. How could you have believed that of me?'

'You were photographed with her.'

'Female company was rare in the outback. That day I chatted to her for just a few minutes. She was a driver on the earth-moving equipment—a woman in a man's world. But when she came onto me, I got away and steered well clear of her after that. Of course, I had no idea Andrew would decide to cause trouble between us.'

'You say cause trouble, he said he was letting us know what you were up to.' This was the story she had lived with for so long. Had she really been tricked?

Jon spat out an expression of disgust. 'And you didn't trust me. You and your family believed him over me. The day after that photo was taken, I was sent out to an exploration site for a month, right out in the desert. The site was just a collection of temporary vans and some water tanks. Mobile phones then weren't what they are now. Besides, there were no communication towers out there. The bosses had satellite phones. We grunts didn't get access to them. I had no idea what was blowing up at home over that photograph.'

'I didn't hear from you. My mother said that spelled guilt.'

'She would say that, wouldn't she? But you knew what communications—or lack of them—were like out there. If you remember, I let you know as soon as I first got there and found out for myself how difficult it was going to be to stay in touch as much as we'd wanted to. Yet you were so eager to blame me. To believe that I would cheat on you. Then when I finally got the chance to defend myself to you, I hit a brick wall.' His face twisted with genuine pain.

'What do you mean?'

'Most of the time when I was able to get in touch, you wouldn't speak to me. And if you did, you didn't seem like you. You were like a different person. You didn't reply to emails. Your mother said you wanted nothing to do with me. Still, when she offered me money to stay with my "mistress" in Australia and leave you alone, I was shocked.'

Natalie stared at him, aghast. 'She what? My mother offered you money to leave me? That can't be true!'

'A substantial sum. You didn't know?'

Natalie shook her head, too stunned to speak. 'I… I had no idea.'

'I didn't take any money from her. Let's make that clear. But if she'd offered to loan us that much to help set us up on our own, I wouldn't have had to go to Australia in the first place. She was out to destroy us, although I didn't realise that back then.'

'I'm reeling here. I had no idea my mother interfered so much in our marriage.'

It couldn't be true. Her mother wouldn't have gone that far. That wasn't the act of a responsible parent. She clutched her head at all the conflicting thoughts ricocheting through her mind. She had never expected to hear this. Back then, who had done the betraying?

'Did you know the divorce was her idea too? She harassed me, telling me that it was in your best interests, and it was what you wanted. That, technically, I had abandoned you. And that no court would give me any access at all to Clem if I didn't cooperate.'

'You believed her?' What web had her parents woven to catch a young couple and set their daughter on the path they'd thought was better for her?

He shrugged. 'I was still young and living in a foreign country. I know there are people who are very savvy in their early twenties. That wasn't me. I was ignorant. My parents didn't really know how to advise me. And they—'

'Thought I'd trapped you. Didn't want to see you dropped out of university and tied down to me.'

'Something like that.' He paused. 'Your mother told me the divorce was your idea.'

'She told me it was what you wanted. That you'd quickly moved on to another woman.'

Natalie put her hands over her face. 'To be honest, a lot of that time is a blur to me. I missed you so much and yet...'

'I missed you too.'

'I was told you cheated on me. I was on a lot of medication. But I know my mother encouraged me not to talk to you.' She stopped to amend herself. 'I believed you cheated on me... now I'm not so sure. I found it hard to believe it of you at the time. Seems like I might have been wrong...very wrong. Jon, tell me again that you didn't cheat on me.'

'I didn't cheat on you. You can be absolutely certain of that.'

'I...believe you. I'm so very sorry I didn't believe you back then. I missed you so desperately yet swung to anger and despair that you had left me. I was in the full throes of postpartum depression then. I didn't know what to think.'

'I don't think any of us understood what we were dealing with.'

'It seems we didn't know what we were dealing with when it came to my mother. I'm horrified, utterly and completely horrified.' Her voice broke.

Jon shook his head. 'I don't get it. I don't understand why she disliked me so much. I did nothing but love her daughter.'

'It was about control. Loss of control, to be more specific. And my dad didn't do anything to stop her. Why do you think Steven lives in Canada now? To get away from them. I defied her by slipping out from under her thumb to go to Durham in the north of England instead of a university closer to home. And what did I do? Fall madly in love with a boy and fall pregnant in my first year. Look, I don't pretend to understand her motivation. That's just my guess.'

'Sounds feasible. Do you think there was an element of punishment in the way she treated us?'

'Could have been. We were so young, thrown into a situation about which we were clueless. I do know we both loved our baby and wanted what was best for her.' She'd thought what had been best for Clem was not to be confused about having two daddies, one who had made a choice to live far away and dropped into her life now and then, and one who was a stable, loving presence in her life every day, always there when she'd needed him.

'Always,' he said.

Natalie paced up and down, then turned back to him. 'You know, when Clem turned eighteen, I thought about our young selves. She's intelligent and has always been mature for her years, but at eighteen she still seemed so young. I couldn't imagine how our daughter would have coped if she'd been thrown into a situation like we were. Not much better, I suspect. But I knew I would never treat her the way my mother treated me. Or treat Tyler, or whoever the hypothetical father might have been, the way she treated you.'

Jon slowly shook his head. 'In hard-won hindsight, I realise I should never have gone to Australia. It was a crazy thing to do.'

'You did it to provide for your family. Not every young guy would be brave enough to do what you did. It was a very grown-up thing to do.'

'That didn't make it any less crazy. I wasn't actually grown up enough to deal with it and the separation from you. My only excuse was that I was desperate to make enough money for us to be independent. Instead, I lost you.'

'I couldn't have been easy to live with back then.' Jon made to protest, but Natalie put up her hand to stop him. 'It's true. Often I wasn't kind to you. I know that. But once I got over the depression and was free of the medication-caused fog, I realised that we would have had options. Surely, we would have been eligible for some kind of benefits as student parents of a baby until we got on our feet.'

'Your mother would have seen that as something which simply wasn't done in her social circle. It would have been seen as a poor reflection on her. That wasn't an option for us.'

Natalie looked up at him. 'So much to think about.'

'And you can have as much time as you need to think about it,' he said.

'So what next?' she said sadly.

'A big hug first,' he said as he pulled her into his arms.

CHAPTER ELEVEN

JON LOOKED DOWN at Natalie, her face tear-stained, make-up smeared around her eyes, her hair ruffled out of place. She looked as emotionally drained as he was. But he felt a new sense of peace about the past. And a stirring of hope for the future. They were very different people now. Could he make it work? He hadn't dared contemplate it until now. *A second chance with Natalie.*

He broke away from the hug. 'I'm sorry for both our younger selves, that we went through all that,' he said. 'All the time that was wasted through no real fault of our own.'

'I… I should apologise on behalf of my parents—'

'Of course you shouldn't. We both suffered. We have to put it behind us. Take this second chance that's been offered to us to—'

'To be friends?' she said.

He looked at her without saying anything

for a long moment. 'There's something I want to make very clear,' he said. 'I don't want to be friends.'

'Oh.' Natalie tensed and began to turn away from him. 'After all the painful details about our past that we've dug up, I... I wouldn't blame if you didn't want to see me any more. But we do have Christmas Day with Clem. We can't let her down and—'

Jon reached down and took both her hands in his, drawing her close again so she had to look up at him. 'That's not what I meant. I meant I want to be more than friends.'

'More than friends?' Her voice was querulous, high pitched.

Was it such a surprise to her? Jon cursed himself for not being clearer about his intentions. 'I want a second chance with you,' he said. 'As in a relationship, not just friendship. I'm making that very clear.'

'You mean, you want to make up for lost time? Remedy past mistakes?'

'That's exactly what I mean.'

'But what if we tried that and it didn't work out? We failed in the past, what makes you think we could make it work again? We're still the same people at heart. What if we crashed and burned again? I don't know that I could deal with that.'

'Admittedly it would be taking a risk,' he acknowledged.

'Perhaps you're more of a risk-taker than I am.'

'There's that,' he said.

'I'm not sure I'm ready to be more than friends, Jon. I don't see how anything more could work. Not with all that pain behind us. I… I'm scarred by it.'

'Maybe we take it step by step?' he suggested. 'It doesn't have to be all or nothing.'

'What do you mean?'

'Natalie Lewis-Grayson-Gibbs, I'm asking you out on a date—as a friend. Nothing more. No expectations.' He gently pushed back a strand of hair that had drifted across her face.

A slow, tentative smile lifted the corners of her mouth. 'You are?'

'Would you like to see *The Nutcracker* with me tonight? With dinner at an excellent Italian restaurant beforehand?'

'I would like that. As friends.' She slid her arms around his waist and he hugged her close. For a long moment he stood there with her in his arms, her curves pressed close against him, rejoicing in her warm closeness, breathing in her sweet floral scent, wanting her. He would have to be patient.

Her voice hitched. 'I'm so sorry my family put you through all that.' Her voice was muffled against his shoulder.

He pulled back so he could see her face. 'Put *us* through all that,' he said. 'And, by the way, my family could have been more supportive, too. They weren't without fault. When I look back, I can't believe we were so easily manipulated.'

'We're looking at it from an adult viewpoint now,' she said. 'Back then we were young. Naïve. Powerless. I didn't have an easy pregnancy and the time after Clem was born wasn't easy either. That said, we should have been able to trust our parents.'

'I thought loving you would be enough to see us through.'

'It should have been. If we'd had the right support.'

'We don't need them now,' he said. 'It's only up to us to make decisions that affect our lives. And to guide Clem if she needs us.' He reminded himself not to push it further than she wanted to take it. 'As friends, I mean.'

'True. Clem has actually asked both of us to help her and Leo with the baby after it's born.'

'She will set the boundaries,' he said.

'And we will do our best,' she said. He realised she referred to them as 'we', which was something new—and gave him a scrap of hope.

'I'm so glad we had that conversation about a past that had affected us so much,' he said.

'And changed the trajectories of our lives,' she said quietly.

Had she been truly happy with Hugo? He wanted to ask, but knew he couldn't.

'Why don't we disperse to our respective bathrooms, freshen up and head out on the town?'

'Good idea,' she said, pulling away from the protective circle of his arms.

'We've finished our "getting to know you phase" and—'

'Was it just a phase?' She looked up at him, her eyes wide.

'I didn't know which way it would go, did you? I believe we both started off hostile to each other but were determined to do our best for Clem, and then—'

She smiled. 'And then we discovered we liked each other—still liked each other, that is.'

He cleared his throat. 'And now we'll be going out to the ballet, as friends.'

He noticed Natalie had to swallow hard before replying. 'And who now have a new knowledge of what went wrong back when we were more than friends.'

'Yes. If only— No. I won't say it. It happened. We can't change that. But now we finally know the truth, we can come to terms with it. You go upstairs. I'll clear up this broken cup.'

She didn't move. 'I remember back then we never left each other without kissing the other goodbye. Even when we left a room. That ritual somehow got lost when we were living with my parents—'

'Because they made fun of us.' Teasing was the explanation from her parents for their mean brand of mockery.

'I didn't remember if we kissed each other goodbye when you left for Australia. Not being able to remember bothered me for a long time. Did we?'

'Of course we did. And I kissed Clementine too.' He'd had to live on the memory of those kisses for a long time.

'Sorry. I'm getting a bit maudlin here,' she said, with a hitch to her voice. She leaned up to kiss him briefly on the cheek. 'I'm going all the way upstairs so am kissing you goodbye.'

She laughed her lovely melodious laugh, and he laughed with her. He liked the feeling it gave him, as if some of the clouds that had darkened their past had been blown away by the breath of an honest conversation. Who knew what it might lead to?

Upstairs in Jon's guest room, Natalie got dressed in somewhat of a tizz. Her heart was racing and her hands trembled, so she had trouble doing up the zip on her dress. Her dress was suitable for going out to the ballet with a person from her past who was more than an acquaintance, but not yet a friend. If she'd anticipated how the compass would swing on their friendship, she would have packed something more glamorous. But, then again, she didn't want to look as if she were trying too hard either. Just friends—no more, no less.

She looked critically at herself in the full-length mirror. She turned this way and that and smoothed the skirt down over her hips. Actually, this dress was okay—and she had never worn it out with Hugo, which, in some way relating to loyalty and rivalry, was important. The soft, deep blue fabric with a thread of silver through it, the wrap bodice and long tight sleeves were elegant without being over the top. It flattered her figure and her colouring. With simple jewellery, her hair tonged into shape, and more make-up than she was used to wearing in recent months, she'd pass muster.

* * *

Jon's reaction told her she'd got it right. He had gone downstairs ahead of her and he watched as she made her way down the open staircase, stepping carefully in high heels. He didn't hide the admiration from his eyes.

'You look absolutely beautiful,' he said when she got close, his eyes narrowed in sensual appraisal. 'I didn't think any woman could be more beautiful than you as a teenager. I was wrong. You, as a mature woman, are off the charts.'

His words warmed her heart. 'Thank you. You look good yourself.'

He was wearing dark trousers and a dark shirt, beautifully cut. Did he always wear dark colours? Why not? He looked hot in them. Really hot. The kisses they'd shared not so long ago were still warm on her lips. How much did she actually want to see *The Nutcracker*? Or could they skip dinner but not miss the ballet and head off to the theatre from here after they—?

She gave herself a mental cold shower. Friends with benefits was not on the agenda.

This date was an occasion to mark a shift in the way she and her ex-husband regarded each other. It shouldn't—couldn't—be rushed.

CHAPTER TWELVE

LONDON AT CHRISTMAS time was even more magical when Natalie was hand in hand with Jon. The lights seemed to twinkle that much more brightly, the snatches of Christmas music drifting from shops and restaurants more beguiling, passers-by more convivial, everyone around them seemed imbued with festive spirit.

Happiness attracts happiness, went the saying. The evening seemed to prove it to be true. Jon had previously been to eat on his own at the Italian restaurant. The staff were delighted that he had brought his beautiful wife to dine with them and neither she nor Jon denied the relationship.

'Fact is, we were once married so why go into lengthy explanations?' Jon said.

What would that explanation be? Natalie thought. How would they explain their situation when she barely understood it herself? But she did know she was just happy to be with Jon—all pretence that they weren't interested in each other had completely dissipated. Being 'just friends' kept things at a distance, but she knew something else was simmering under the surface.

She loved Italian food, but she pushed her delicious tagliatelle around on her plate, scarcely taking a bite. It was too excitingly unnerving to be seated opposite Jon, not worrying if their knees nudged or their hands grazed. In fact she welcomed every touch, no matter how slight. With this level of sensual tension humming away, how might the evening end? Was it possible to be friends with benefits without it ending in disaster?

It was the same at the ballet. *The Nutcracker* was a favourite, and she enjoyed the ballet company's interpretation of the classic tale of young Clara being transported to the kingdom of the nutcracker to join in the battle against the evil mouse king. In the friendship group she'd shared with Hugo, ballet was seen as something for only women to enjoy. She'd not once attended a ballet with Hugo. But Jon was interested in both dance and music. He'd been such a good dancer back then. She shivered a little at the memories—the man had rhythm. Again, she thought about and discarded the idea of suggesting they sing some carols for Clem on Christmas Day. Would that be pushing it for her and Jon and Clem?

But under their conversation over dinner, their after-performance critique of the ballet, bubbled anticipation of what might happen once they were alone in Jon's apartment. Was it too soon? But they'd lost so much time together, what was the point of waiting to go to bed with Jon? Actually, they'd never bothered about it having to be a bed. A sofa, the back seat of a car, it had never mattered to either of them. They'd just wanted each other. She shook her head to clear her thoughts—she'd insisted they stick to being friends. It was the wisest option. *But she wanted him.* She was kidding herself that friendship would suffice.

The last time she'd made love with Jon she'd had no idea it would not happen again. It had been the night before he'd flown to Australia. Their lovemaking had been as fulfilling as it had always been for them since they'd got together. The spats and snaps and misunderstandings they'd been having had been forgotten as they'd enjoyed giving and taking pleasure with each other. They'd fallen asleep in each other's arms until Clem had woken them, wailing, at some ungodly hour. She remembered it was he who had got up to Clem. He'd been such a good father.

That long-ago Natalie would have laughed out loud if someone had told her that was the last time she would make love with her husband. Or that she would end up divorced from him and married to another man. And that for the next twenty-plus years she would long for the ecstasy she had shared with Jay Jay.

After the ballet, she and Jon walked home to his apartment from the theatre, hand in hand. It was chilly, their breaths fogging in the cold, and she secretly hoped for snow on Christmas Day.

They unlinked hands to stand discreetly apart in the foyer of the building. There were security cameras. Once inside the elevator they smiled at each other. Questions were asked and answered without a word being spoken. Natalie raised her eyes to the security cameras in there too. She had no desire to be captured on camera kissing her ex-husband, and his rueful expression let her know he thought so too. In their forties and kissing like horny teenagers was a big deal—even if they'd once used to be those horny teenagers. Because it was a prelude for something more than kisses she'd been thinking about—no, longing for—all evening.

It was up to her—she knew Jon was waiting for her consent.

There was another security camera mounted on the wall outside Jon's apartment. He waved at it. 'No cameras inside,' he said to Natalie.

She scarcely heard him, she was so eager to get inside and slam the door behind them. At last. She and Jon together and alone. He closed the door and turned to her. Their eyes met. He didn't say anything, he didn't need to. She read the question in his eyes and sent an answer to him. *Yes*. She wanted him as she'd wanted him their first time together, she wanted him as she'd never stopped wanting him through their brief marriage, she wanted him as she'd fantasised about having him all those years. Only that had been Jay Jay, and this was Jon. How different would the very grown-up Jon be as her lover?

He took a step towards her and she met him halfway. She unbuttoned his coat and pushed it away, impatient when it caught on his shoulders. He shrugged it off so it fell to the floor. She wound her arms around his neck and pulled him close for a proper kiss, immediately passionate, immediately demanding. Desire flooded through her. She broke away, and shrugged off her expensive designer coat. She didn't care if it fell on the floor, she just wanted fewer barriers between her and Jon.

'You're so sexy in that dress,' he said, his voice hoarse. 'I've been wanting you, wanting this, all evening.'

'Me too.' Her voice broke. 'Wanting you so much.'

He pulled her tighter as he kissed her again, urgent, demanding, and she pressed her body to his. Her breasts to the solid wall of his chest, hips to the hardness of his thighs. Did his body feel the same as that last time? Those many times before the last time? This felt both familiar and excitingly new. His chest was broader and more muscular, his arms strong and powerful.

He caressed her back, then down the side of her breast and she arched her back in pleasure. She got the feeling he was remembering her body, perhaps discovering she was softer in places, stronger in others from regular Pilates and visits to the gym.

His hands felt so good on her body—they always had. Immediately she melted for him. She—a virgin at eighteen—had gone to bed with him on their first date. He'd wanted to wait once he knew it would be her first time, but she hadn't wanted to wait. He'd been The

One. And she hadn't regretted it, not for a second. Looking back, she realised they should have been a bit more careful with contraception. How different their lives might have been if they had been. But then she wouldn't have had Clem—and Clem was everything to her.

Clem. Contraception. She pulled away from Jon. 'Er, this is awkward, but I could still get pregnant and I don't want to.'

'I'll take care of protection,' he said gruffly.

They continued to kiss and explore each other's bodies over their clothes, their breathing becoming ragged and urgent. Her body ached to be closer to his—close, closer, as close as she could possibly be. With impatient fingers she tugged his shirt from his trousers to slide her hands up across his bare warm back. He groaned and the sound of his arousal aroused her even more.

'Sofa?' she managed to pant out.

'Bed,' he said.

He swooped her up into his arms. 'Really?' she said. 'Up those stairs?'

'Easy,' he said.

She kicked off her shoes and snuggled in close. He effortlessly carried her up the open staircase and kicked open his bedroom door.

Natalie scarcely noticed what the bedroom

looked like, but she got an impression of the same kind of contemporary design as the rest of the apartment, an enormous bed, subtle lighting. They fell together on the bed, laughing as they landed.

Jon found the zip at the back of her dress and had it down in seconds and the dress entirely off in another few seconds. She was left in her underwear and sheer tights. Tights—how seriously unsexy for a woman intent on seduction. She'd thought that when she was putting them on earlier in the evening but had gone ahead and worn them anyway because it was cold outside. Maybe that was the difference between age eighteen and age forty-three. She tugged at the waistband, but Jon took over.

'Let me do that,' he said. He made pulling down a pair of tights into an extended caress, taking his time to kiss her belly and thighs on the way down. She shuddered with pleasure at each new sensitive place he teased with his lips and tongue. By the time he got to her toes she was aching with desire, her hips bucking towards him.

He started to play with the front fastening of her lacy bra, and she thrust her breasts, nipples aching with want, forward for his attention.

But, with a great effort of will, she stopped him. 'Let's get you undressed first.'

'I'm up for that,' he said, flinging himself on his back in mock surrender.

She laughed and unbuttoned his shirt and slid it off his shoulders. Her laughter faded and her breath caught at the magnificence that met her greedy gaze. Yes, his chest was more developed from when he was younger, tanned, rippling with muscle, his arms powerful. A dusting more of body hair, perhaps. He was exceptionally fit. Gym? Weights? He probably swam too—he'd always liked to swim and had swum for the university swimming club. No doubt he had his own pool in Perth with sunshine all year round. Whatever he did it worked—he was hot.

She wanted to tear off his trousers, just rip them down the seams to get them off as soon as possible. But he might not appreciate that, they seemed very expensive. He was probably nowhere near as desperate for her as she was for him. Her need to get him naked made her hands tremble and she fumbled with his belt buckle. She cursed under her breath. Jon laughed. She realised how ridiculous she was being, and she laughed too, albeit self-consciously.

'Let me help,' he said as he quickly undid the buckle. He went to unfasten his trousers, but she pushed his hand aside.

'I'll do that,' she said as she undid the button and pulled down the zip.

She pulled down his trousers to reveal the unmistakable evidence of his desire for her. Impressive. Very impressive. Her breath caught.

Jon groaned. 'Don't linger, Natalie. Don't tease me like I teased you. I want to make sure I last for the main act.'

She did too, so it was in her interests to take heed. Still, once she'd got his trousers off, she couldn't resist tugging his boxers down with her teeth, over his hips and legs. She enjoyed having him under her sensual control.

'Natalie,' he warned. 'You're torturing me.'

'And you're enjoying it, by the sound of it,' she teased.

He made a deep, sensual growl in his throat. He used to do that when he was really aroused. It turned her on now just as it had then.

He flipped her over on her back, and gave his attention to her bra, unclipping it so her breasts were bared to him, and he kissed and caressed them, tonguing one nipple while he rolled the other between thumb and finger. Just as he'd used to arouse her, but it wasn't quite the same, as the soft brush of his beard added a new level of sensual pleasure. Oh yes, he remembered what pleased her, what moved her to ecstasy. She remembered too, what had pleased him then. She had never forgotten. His clever fingers moved downwards to where she ached for his touch. He knew just how to get her ready for him, to have her bucking her hips in a silent plea for possession. Shivers of anticipation ran down her spine. *Her man.*

He didn't ask was she ready, he didn't have to. Her murmurs of pleasure and need did that. He only paused to put on protection. At last he pushed inside her, that confident, hard, exciting possession, just as she had remembered, had longed for, for so many years. She loved his rhythmic strokes, the intimacy of being joined with him, of pleasure so intense as it built to a peak that it had her convulsing around him and crying out his name—Jon.

Even in her passion-fogged urgency, she realised that she had not called out for Jay Jay. This was about Jon. Here. Now. The same but different. The present not the past. He let her wallow in the utter pleasure of it, before he started thrusting into her again until she came once more. Only then did he strive for his release, and she loved the groan of intense pleasure he made when he came, immediately familiar yet excitingly new.

As she lay there in his arms, replete, her breathing slowly returning to normal, she found herself drifting to sleep but she fought it, wanting to prolong these moments of utter fulfilment. And the joy, the utter joy that she was back with him. But there was sadness too. She couldn't stop a tear from escaping and rolling down her cheek, a slight convulsive sob she fought unsuccessfully to suppress. With their bodies so intimately close, Jon couldn't fail to notice.

'Hey, are you okay?'

'Fine,' she said with another betraying sniffle.

'You don't sound fine.'

'I am fine, more than fine, it's just that I can't help thinking—'

He propped himself on his elbow so he looked down into her face. 'About all the time we've missed out on?'

She nodded as another tear rolled down her cheek. Jon gently wiped it away with his thumb. Why did she keep crying when she should be ecstatic about what had happened between them? She never cried. Being with Jon had opened some kind of emotional floodgate.

'Me too,' he said.

'Why did we let it go? What we had together, I mean?'

'Other people's interference,' he said, anger lacing his voice. 'Exacerbated by the incredible distance and poor telecommunications.'

'After hearing what you told me, I never want to speak to my mother again,' she stated. 'Not that I speak to her much anyway. She's been less than helpful in her advice about how I should bring up Clem.' She paused. 'But we should have been stronger, fought harder, sought help outside our families.'

'All that,' he said. 'I've thought about it often over the years. But circumstances were against us. What if we'd been left to struggle on our own? Would we have done any better?'

'I think we would have.'

'Or we might have gone under.'

She thought back to the outbursts and squabbles that had marred their last weeks and months together. 'Maybe.'

'But we'll never know, will we?' he said. 'And we have to accept that.'

She took a deep breath. 'You're right. Angsting over what ifs and what might have beens won't get us anywhere.'

'While being thankful for a second chance might get us—'

'Enjoying every minute and coming back for more,' she said as she twisted into his arms again. 'Are you up for it?'

'Is that a challenge?' He laughed as he pulled her close and let her know he was very much up for that challenge.

Jon woke early the next morning from a deep sleep. For a moment he was disorientated—that was often the case, as he travelled so often for work. He could be waking up in Brazil or South Africa or the Australian outback. But he was in his bedroom in his London apartment. He'd been dreaming about Natalie, as he sometimes had over the years. Then he realised, with a rush of heartfelt emotion, that it hadn't been a dream. Natalie was lying asleep next to him.

Weak winter sunlight filtered through the high, factory windows. It picked up golden glints in her hair, spread across the pillow. The same glorious red hair she had given to their daughter. The room was warm, and she had thrown off the bedclothes to reveal pale arms and shoulders, the curve of her breasts. His heart seemed to miss a beat. She was even lovelier than she had been at eighteen when he had fallen instantly in love with her.

At the time he hadn't questioned that head-long tumble into love and commitment—just believed that what he'd found with Natalie was for life and his future would be linked with hers. Sadly—tragically, when he thought about it—his eyes had been opened to what could go wrong when a person's life turned completely upside down. Now he'd heard the truth about his split from Natalie and Clem, he never wanted anything to do with her parents again—he wasn't sure he'd be able to restrain himself. Even if they were Clem's grandparents.

Was this reunion with Natalie simply a scratching of an old itch—or something more profound? She had such a complete life here now, whereas his was more peripatetic, with constant travel and no real ties to anywhere, except that Australia was his home base. What might Natalie want from him? What could he give her?

Was there a place for him in Natalie's life as being anything more than her daughter's father? They had made love, and it had been every bit as wonderful as it had been when they were younger. But he wanted more. Not just sex. He wanted her in his life, by his side. For how long he didn't know—preferably for ever. It was early days to be thinking that far ahead. But he sure as hell wanted to try to secure her. Not everyone was given a second chance. He wanted to see if they could start again and move forward. It might or might not work out with her—they were different people now. He was aware of that. But he wouldn't know if they didn't give a new relationship a chance.

He had missed out on her twenties and her thirties, but Natalie's forties and more stretched ahead of her—possibly with him. He didn't want to miss out on further years with her.

He had never imagined this would happen, this reunion with his former wife. He had gone to that first meeting at the park determined to do anything in his power to strengthen his newly revived relationship with his daughter. Anger towards Natalie had still simmered under his polite conversation. At the time he hadn't known how angry she, in turn, still was towards him for his so-called infidelity and betrayal. Yet despite that, the old attraction had been too powerful to be ignored. And he had found himself slipping back into the enjoyment of her company—as he had never enjoyed another woman's company.

He wondered now if that was the reason he had never had a satisfactory long-term relationship—no other woman could match Natalie. His second wife had accused him of never having got over his first. He had vehemently denied it, but perhaps she'd made a valid point. And now he'd found his first wife again, he didn't want to lose her.

Natalie stirred and stretched out her limbs luxuriously. He watched as her eyes flickered open. There was a moment of surprise followed by pleasure and delight. 'So, you're not a dream,' she murmured as she reached out a hand to put on his arm—he was real. She smiled. 'It's really you, naked and next to me, Jonathan James Grayson.'

'All present and correct,' he said.

'Thank you for last night,' she murmured.

'Thank you,' he replied.

'The dinner and the ballet were good too,' she said, a knowing smile curving her lips.

'They were,' he admitted. 'But not as good as what came after.'

'Agreed,' she said, moving closer, dropping a kiss on his shoulder. 'We're brilliant together.'

'We always were.'

'From our very first time.'

'I don't want to let you go again, Natalie,' he said, his voice rough with emotion.

'I don't have to go home until after the musical tomorrow night. Freddie is with my neighbour until then.'

'I don't mean that.' He cupped her face in his hands. 'I don't mean just today. I mean tomorrow and tomorrow and tomorrow after that. We've got more than twenty years apart to make up for.'

She tilted her head to the side. 'Do you really feel that way?'

'Very much so,' he said.

'Thank heaven,' she said. 'Because I do too. It's…well, it seems to me like a gift that we've been given a second chance. Let's grab it with both hands and see what happens.' She went quiet for a moment. 'But we're different people now. Burdened with scars and baggage. Maybe the old magic won't ignite again. But it was there for me last night and I'm more than willing to give it a go. And if it fizzles out, at least we know we tried.'

'Count me in,' he said hoarsely.

She kissed him, a brief, sweet kiss. 'Me too, and with no one interfering this time,' she added.

'Shall we tell Clem?' he asked. 'That we're going to try again, I mean?'

Natalie smiled. 'You mean, you think she might interfere? She would most certainly have her own strong opinions. But I don't want to be influenced by my darling daughter either. So, I don't think we should tell her. Not yet, anyway.'

'In that case I don't think we should tell anyone at all,' he said.

'Good idea. I especially don't want anyone in my family to know we're giving it a try.'

'With your parents in Spain and your brother in Canada that seems unlikely.'

'If…if it doesn't work out for us no one need know. We'll be spared the commiserations.'

'Fair enough.'

'I… I don't think it's a good idea if we're seen together in Guildford. I know a lot of people there and anyway—'

'I have no interest in seeing the house where you lived with Hugo.' He couldn't think of anything worse. Wisely or not, he just didn't want to think about that time of her life where she'd existed completely without him.

'I understand that.'

He lay back against the pillow and she rested her head on his shoulder with his arm encircling her. 'Were you happy with Hugo? Did you love him?' He held his breath for her answer.

It took her a few beats. 'He was a good man, and I had a good life with him.' She paused again. 'He was a loving father to Clem and she loved him.'

She still hadn't said if she'd loved Hugo, but Jon couldn't press her. He probably shouldn't have asked her. He couldn't bear to hear Natalie tell him Hugo had been the love of her life.

Deep down he still believed Hugo, in cahoots with Natalie's parents, had stolen his wife. Then Hugo had triumphed further and won Clem away from him—with Natalie on the sidelines not protesting. Jon had been gutted when, at age thirteen, Clem had informed him she didn't want to see him any more, at all. Just at the time when he'd had more opportunity and finances to see more of her. He would never admit it to Natalie but there were occasions when he'd been visiting the UK when he'd gone to Clem's school at pick-up time, mingling anonymously with the crowd of other parents, just to catch a glimpse of his teenage daughter.

Natalie took a deep breath. 'Shall we say I soon realised I had to dial down my expectations of marriage to Hugo. There…there was never any real passion between us. I had no independence. No career of my own. But I did grow to care for him very much.'

'Fair enough.' He hated the thought of her merely existing with boring old Hugo.

Jon forced his voice into the range of reasonable. 'I'm glad he was good to Clem, at least.' And was secretly pleased he hadn't given Natalie the orgasms he gave her so easily. Or, indeed, a child.

It was as if she'd read his mind. 'If it makes you feel better, I never went to a ballet or a musical or a rock concert with Hugo, because he didn't have a musical bone in his body. It was dinner parties and worthy plays, and Clem's school concerts and speech nights, visits to the world's most boring parents-in-law, and gardening on the weekend.'

'So he wasn't the love of your life?' he said, knowing he wasn't succeeding in keeping the jealousy from his voice.

'I think you know who the love of my life was,' she said, her voice hitching.

And will be again, Jon vowed to himself.

She lifted herself up and kissed him on the mouth. 'Can we keep Hugo out of our bedroom and concentrate on us?'

'Absolutely,' Jon said. That was just what he wanted to hear.

'Let's spend the day in bed making love and watching TV and ordering take-out food to be delivered,' Natalie said. 'We can catch up on some of the lazy days and relaxed home times we were cheated of. Then we can dress up and go out to the musical tonight as planned.'

'Sounds like an excellent plan,' he said. Could there possibly be a better one?

'I've had another thought. Do you have your guitar here?'

'Not the one I had when we were at uni. That's in Perth. But I do have a guitar here.'

'What say we surprise Clem by singing a few Christmas carols on Christmas Day?'

'I wasn't expecting that,' he said.

'Is it such a bad thought?'

'It's a long time since we've sung together. We'll need to practise.'

'Do you think we could do it again?'

'I suspect we could. We won't know until we try.'

'Let's try, then. I think Clem would like it.' She paused. 'I would like it.'

'I would like it too,' he agreed. 'I'll tune the guitar this afternoon. Any carols in particular?'

'I think "Silent Night" might be nice for Clem—you know, "mother and child".'

'I have a yen for "God Rest Ye Merry, Gentlemen".'

'"Away in a Manger" is another good one for an expectant mother.'

He laughed. 'Keep in mind Clem's only twenty-four. I reckon she'd like "All I Want for Christmas Is You". Or something more rousing, anyway.'

'And of course we'll wear our sequinned Santa hats.'

'Will we?' He laughed. 'Why not?'

Jon had a feeling that, with Natalie involved, Christmas at Clem's might be livelier than he had imagined. He was looking forward to it. If he and Natalie sang as harmoniously as they had when they were younger, might Clem guess they were more to each other again now? That might be a good way to introduce their new relationship. Personally, he wanted to sing 'All I Want for Christmas Is You' because that was the truth of it for him. Being with Natalie and Clem would be the best Christmas present of all, with the bonus of a grandbaby to come in the new year.

'Good,' Natalie said. 'That's sorted, then. Tomorrow, you can drive me back home and wait while I pick up Freddie, and pack up more clothes. Then we'll come back here and I'll stay with you until Christmas Day when we go to Clem's.'

'And after that?' He couldn't hide the raw hunger from his voice.

'By then I think we'll be clear on where we want to go with this,' she said. He realised neither of them had addressed the elephant in the room—the big one wearing an outsized custom-made, red sequinned Santa hat. If this reunion worked out there was the inescapable fact to consider that he lived in Australia where his business and interests lay. She lived in England, where all her interests lay. Who would have to compromise?

CHAPTER THIRTEEN

WHAT ABOUT AFTER Christmas Day? What would happen then? The following day, by the time Natalie was dressed in the jeans and jacket she'd worn to Hampton Court Palace, ready to head back home to pick up Freddie, she was very sure about where she wanted to go with Jon. All the way. Full-on commitment. In his life again as his wife—whether or not they formalised it with an actual second marriage ceremony.

Back then, when she'd been eighteen, she'd made up her mind about Jay Jay very quickly. It was no different now. She and Jon belonged together. They should never have been apart. No questions asked. She was, in fact, terrified of losing him again. She didn't know how she'd manage a second time.

But while there were no questions about her commitment—and although they hadn't actually spoken about it, she believed Jon felt the same—there were questions about how they might manage a future together. The biggest question to be answered was about where they would live. His home was in Western Australia, the other side of the world in a country she had never even visited, let alone contemplated living there. The place where Jon had disappeared to all those years ago. Back then there had been times she'd hated Australia and had vowed never to go there. She lived in Guildford, in a house she would never want to live in with Jon and yet it was Clem's childhood home, her safety net.

Clem. Her daughter was the main issue. Clem was about to embark on a life as a mother and she needed her own mother. Her father too. Clem had asked both her parents for help.

Clem would need help not just around the time of the birth and caring for a newborn, but also when her baby was older. Bringing up a child was tough—rewarding but tough—even with two parents. Clem had a career she would need to maintain. Natalie wanted to help her as much as she could, on her daughter's terms, not the way her own mother had 'helped' her and Jon all the way to the divorce court. When it boiled down to it, Natalie would be there when Clem needed her. On call. She could give no less.

But how did that fit in with the love of her life back on the scene with his home being on the other side of the world?

'Ready?' Jon asked.

'Just about,' she said. 'I'm just looking around checking what I need to make Freddie comfortable here. I might need to buy him a few things. And remind me, when we get back here, I need to find where the nearest parks are. Oh, and while I'm thinking about shopping—'

'As you do,' said Jon, swinging her into his arms for a swift hug and an affectionate kiss dropped on the top of her head.

She laughed. 'Well, yes. That's me. But seriously, we need to get something Christmassy for this apartment. Maybe after we get back from Guildford, we could pop down to the South Bank Christmas market and buy one of those cute little trees that come already decorated and—'

'Whatever you want,' he said, indulgently. 'You can string this place with lights and decorations from rafter to floor as far as I'm concerned. As long as you're here with me, I don't mind how Christmassy you make it.'

'Hmm, okay, you're giving me carte blanche, you say?' She smiled teasingly as she looked around, exaggerating a search of places to lavishly decorate.

'Now I'm getting worried,' he said, with a mock frown.

Natalie laughed again. As she did, she realised she had laughed more with Jon in these few days than she could remember doing over the last two years. 'Seriously, no cause for concern. The beauty of this place is in its stark simplicity. Just a small tree will do. For this year anyway—' She realised what she had said and faltered to a halt.

He looked down into her face. 'We need to talk about next year. Where we'll be, how we'll manage the distance between where we both live now.'

She took his hand and gripped it tightly. 'Yes. We do need to talk. I want to be with you, you know that, don't you?'

'And I with you. I told you, I don't want to let you go.'

They shared a swift, sweet kiss.

'It all revolves around Clem,' Natalie said. 'I know she has something going on with Leo, but he's not the baby's father and anything might happen. We're the only people in her life who can be there for her the way she needs for the motherhood journey she's about to embark on.

She has Tyler's parents, too, yes, but it's her own parents she needs most. Her mother—'

'And her father,' Jon said firmly.

'We… I…am tied to her. I have to put her first.' As she had when she'd agreed to marry Hugo. In truth, there was no sacrifice she wouldn't make for her daughter.

'We have options. We can work it out.'

'I… I'm scared if you go back to Australia without me, I… I'll never see you again. Like… like last time. I couldn't bear that, Jon.'

He pulled her to him in a tight hug. 'Me neither. I couldn't bear it either. Last time was hell on both of us.' He pulled back and looked into her face. 'Communication. This time we'll get it right.' He paused. 'We'll have an hour in the car, let's talk it over then. Most likely the first of many talks.'

'Good idea. I'm ready to go,' she said.

She went to pick up her handbag from the table just as her phone inside it started to ring. 'That's probably my neighbour calling to confirm the time I'll be picking up Freddie.' She burrowed in her bag and found her phone. She looked at the screen and frowned. 'I don't know this number.'

'Don't answer it,' said Jon as he shrugged on his coat.

Natalie put her phone back in her bag. It rang again. 'I think I should answer it,' she said. 'You never know…' Later, Natalie would be so glad she'd picked the phone up that second time.

'Hello. Yes.'

Natalie listened carefully to the midwife from Kensington hospital. She could feel the colour draining from her face with every word. Finally, she disconnected the phone with fingers that barely worked. She turned to Jon.

'What's wrong?' he demanded.

'It…it's Clem. That was a midwife. Clem's been admitted to hospital with pre-eclampsia. It's a complication of pregnancy. She's being kept in for…for observation and monitoring.' Her voice broke on the last words.

As she spoke Jon was looking up pre-eclampsia on his phone. He read out his findings. 'Pre-eclampsia is characterised by persistent undiagnosed high blood pressure, protein in the urine, swelling of the face, hands and feet.' He looked across at Natalie. 'It's potentially dangerous to both mother and baby.'

Natalie put her hand to her heart. 'She's only thirty-four and a half weeks pregnant.'

'That's too early to—'

'Yes. It is. Far too early. Oh, how has this

happened? Clem has looked after herself brilliantly, and she was fine at all her pre-natal check-ups. I saw her three days ago and she looked fine, although I did notice she seemed tired.'

'According to this website, pre-eclampsia can't be predicted.'

'She's been so healthy, I don't understand it.'

'Come on. We have to get to the hospital. Clem needs us. We might get some answers there.'

They were at the door and in the lift in seconds. Natalie urged the lift to go down faster. 'Thank heaven we're not in Guildford, with at least an hour's drive to get to the hospital,' she said.

'From here, we should be there in less than twenty minutes.'

They ran to where the car was parked. Jon took off with a squeal of tyres. 'I'll get us there as fast as I can.' Mentally, Natalie urged him to go even faster.

Natalie picked up her phone. 'I should phone Tyler's parents, Fiona and Gary,' she said, punching out their number. 'They'll want to be there too.'

She spoke to Fiona, who was shocked, and

told Natalie she and Gary would be at the hospital as soon as they could.

'Don't forget to call your neighbour about Freddie,' Jon said.

'I'll do it now.' She spoke briefly to her neighbour, who knew Clem well. 'She said she's happy to keep Freddie with her as long as I need her to. She sends best wishes to Clem.'

'Good, at least you don't have to worry about Freddie,' Jon said.

Natalie realised she was wringing her hands together on her lap. She answered on a half-sob. 'Yes, it just leaves my mind free to worry myself sick about my daughter.'

'I'm worried too. But she's at the hospital, in good hands. And we'll be there very soon.'

CHAPTER FOURTEEN

NATALIE HAD THE car door open ready to hop out as soon as Jon stopped the car to drop her at the hospital. 'Meet you there,' she said as she slammed the car door behind her. Jon drove off to park the car. She had to get to Clem.

She made her way to the maternity unit and was directed to the visitors' waiting room, where she waited, anxiously tapping her foot. She scarcely noticed where staff had added festive touches even to this pedestrian hospital environment—tinsel festoons, glass bowls of multicoloured baubles, cards. She'd never given it much thought, but assumed they couldn't decorate the sterile parts of the hospital. And staff would have to be on duty all over the holidays.

She didn't have to wait long before Clem's midwife came out and called her name. Natalie jumped to her feet.

'Can I see Clem? I—'

'I'm afraid not, Mrs Gibbs. Clementine suffered a seizure not long after I spoke to you. She was sent straight to Theatre and is scheduled for a caesarean section—'

'A seizure? My daughter had a seizure?' Natalie felt as though her heart had stopped.

'Fortunately, while under our observation.'

'You're taking the baby out now by C-section? Even though she's had a seizure? Even though she's only thirty-four and a half weeks—she's not ready to—'

'The only cure for eclampsia is to deliver the baby,' the midwife said firmly. 'She's in very good hands, I assure you.'

'She wanted a natural birth and—'

'Our priority is to save the life of both mother and baby.'

The midwife's words served to sober Natalie out of her worry-induced panic. 'Of course. And I'm grateful. But the baby will be very premature.'

'As soon as the baby is born it will be taken to our neonatal intensive care unit. Baby will get the care he or she needs and will stay there until it's safe to take him or her home.'

'I'm thankful for that, but I'm so worried about my daughter. She…she's my only child. She needs me.'

The midwife put a reassuring hand on her arm. 'I understand. I will be with her. We will keep you in touch with what's happening.'

At that moment, Jon rushed into the visitors' room. Natalie introduced him to the midwife as Clementine's father. Jon started to ask a question, but the midwife interrupted him. 'I have to go to your daughter. Your wife will fill you in. And we will keep you informed.'

'Thank you,' Natalie said. 'You've been very helpful.'

'What did she say?' asked Jon.

'I'll catch you up,' said Natalie. 'Let's find somewhere to sit.'

She was aware of his concern too. Out of the rows of institutional chairs with padded blue seats and backs, they managed to find two spots that gave them a degree of privacy.

Natalie sat next to Jon, gripping his hand as she told him what the midwife said.

'She's having the baby today?' he said.

'That's right.'

'But she's not due until the end of January.'

'The thirtieth, if she'd made it full term.'

'Let me look that up,' he said, getting his phone out.

'Seriously?' she said. 'Do you always do this?'

'It's better to know than worry over the unknown,' he said. He scanned his screen for several minutes then looked back up to her. 'The news is good. I've checked several reliable sources. The opinion seems to be that a nearly thirty-five-week-premature baby has an excellent chance of not just surviving but thriving.'

'That's a relief,' she said.

'Not only that but they're less likely to have any of the severe problems that can be associated with a very premature baby.'

She squeezed his hand. 'Thanks to Dr Internet for the reassurance. But I'll feel happier when I hear it from Clem's doctor.'

'We'll just wait here for as long as we have to. That's all we can do.'

Natalie twisted in her seat to face him. 'Thank you for being here with me. I'd hate to be going through this by myself.'

'I told you, I'm here to help you and Clem wherever I can. Although, where's Leo? I thought he might be here.'

'I don't know. But I appreciate that you're with me. Clem will too.' She paused. 'You know, I've thought about this a lot over the last few days. Since…since we got back together. I mean seriously. As a couple. I've wondered how we were going to make a relationship work when we live on opposite sides of the world.'

'We were going to talk about it on the way to your house.'

'I guess we could talk about it now. Quietly, that is. I don't want anyone to overhear us.'

'Understood,' he said. 'I suspect we'll be here for quite a while.'

'This… Clem…has shaken me.'

'It's scary stuff,' he said. 'I'm worried too.'

She sighed. 'If I thought before that my priority was to be here for Clem as she navigated parenthood, I'm even more determined now.'

'You've always put her first, as a mother should.'

'But to put her first, I have to be here. What if I hadn't been here today? What if I'd been, say, in Australia when I got that call from the midwife? That seventeen-hour flight home you mentioned would be seventeen hours too long in an emergency.'

'I can't argue with that. Australia suffers from the tyranny of distance.'

She thought for a long moment. 'How important is it for you to live in Perth?'

He didn't hesitate with his reply. 'Very important. My business is headquartered there. Some of the mines I have an interest in are in

Western Australia. I make my living—one way or the other—from mining, Natalie.'

'So many people work remotely these days.'

He shook his head. 'Not possible for me. Not in the long term. Not if I want to keep making the kind of money I make.'

'Do you need to do that?'

Jon looked at her as if that were a ridiculous question. 'I'm forty-four. Nowhere near retirement age. Nor do I want to retire.' He kept his voice low. 'Those early years scarred me in more ways than one. I couldn't keep my wife and child because I didn't have any money.'

'You were barely out of your teens.'

'And a husband and father who felt his responsibilities keenly. I couldn't provide for you and Clem, and I lost you. I put up with so much crap from your parents, and I still lost you. I vowed never to be poor again. Fortunately for me, I landed in an industry where, with enough smarts, hard work and intuition, it was possible to make a lot of money quickly. The more I made, the more I invested. I got a taste for it, making money, I mean. It assuaged the hollow left by the loss of my wife and child. I can't stop now, Natalie.'

'You mean you're addicted to wealth?'

'If you put it that way.'

'So that virtually cuts out any chance of us living together,' she said dully.

'It shouldn't have to. That kind of money makes things easier too. I travel a lot. But I can cut down my time in Perth to spend more time in the UK. Ideally, you could come and spend time in Perth. Fly first class. You'd like it there.'

'But I can't be that far away from Clem. Ever. What if she needs me? What if things don't work out with Leo? What if something went wrong with her and the baby and I was a seventeen-hour flight away? And that seventeen hours doesn't count the travelling time between airport and home. You don't fly any faster in first class. The truth has hit me fair and square. She's lost Hugo, lost Tyler, her grandparents aren't on the scene and this thing with Leo, whatever it is, is brand new. I mean, he's not even here right now. I can't leave her. She only has me she can completely rely on.'

'And me.'

'Only when you're in London.'

'You mean you can't see a way this can ever work? You and me, I mean.'

'At the moment, no.' She paused. 'Not that I don't want it to work; I desperately do want it to work.'

'There must be a way around this.'

'Can you see it? I can't,' she said. 'All the compromise would be on my side. Again.'

'What do you mean "again"?'

'It was me who was left behind while you flew away. I missed you so much I don't think I could go through that pain again. Then you never came back.'

'And now we know why,' he said grimly.

'It doesn't take away the pain of all those years without you,' she countered.

'Next time, you come with me.'

'But if I go with you, I'll worry about Clem being on her own.'

Natalie felt dismayed as she and Jon sank into a grim silence. Why did she have to bring this up now? This was her fault. But she couldn't see a way to make it work. She had compromised so much in her life—in particular, her marriage to Hugo—but she couldn't compromise when it came to Clem.

She had awoken this morning so blissfully happy to be back with Jon. It had all seemed perfect yesterday, reunited, a beautiful future with the only man she'd ever loved. But now it seemed almost impossible to have that future. And this emergency with Clem only exacerbated it.

Jon took Natalie's hand and squeezed it. She squeezed it back. Such a simple thing, holding hands with your man. But could he be her man? Would his need to live in Australia and her need to be with her daughter end this reunion before it had had time to develop?

'Listen,' he said. 'This is such a stressful time for us.'

'I can only imagine how our darling daughter is feeling.'

'Yes, but you're with her all the way and she'll know you're here.'

Natalie sniffed. 'You, too.'

'Yes, me too. But I can't pretend to be as important to her at this time as her mum.'

She nodded. 'Thank you.'

'I heard everything you said about your commitment to Clem and what that means to us for our future as a couple. How we might not be able to make it work. The mines in Western Australia operate largely on a fly-in-fly-out basis, FIFO they call it. The workers—usually men because of the manual nature of so many of the jobs—are flown onto a remote site with basic accommodation where they work long shifts, twelve hours a day. They work for seven days or fourteen days in a row, then fly back to their families for seven days or fourteen days of leisure, depending on distance.'

'The wives and families are on their own while hubby is away working?'

'That's right.'

'It sounds disruptive for the families.'

'It is, but not as disruptive as locating families on far-flung remote mining sites, which are often temporary, with minimal facilities and no provision for children. It's not ideal but financially the rewards are excellent, and people put up with it because of that. It's never thought of as long-term.'

She frowned. 'And you're telling me this because…?'

'Maybe we could consider a kind of FIFO arrangement where I fly to Perth and back while you stay in the UK, where you can be available for Clem.'

'It's a possibility, I suppose, but I can't say I like it. Every time you flew to Australia, I'd fear you wouldn't be coming back.'

'But I would come back on a specified date. I can't say I like it either, but we might have to compromise to be together.'

Together for some of the time, that was. Was that what she wanted? Could she bear it? Or was it all or nothing with her and Jon? She wanted the *all* but couldn't bear the idea of the *nothing*. And she still wasn't sure that being with each other part-time could work.

'It's an idea to consider,' she said reluctantly.

'Now isn't the time to be making those decisions, but we could think about it. Or maybe come up with a better idea.'

'I promise to think about it.' She turned to him. 'I really want to make this work for all of us, Clem included.'

Jon kissed her. 'We don't have to rush into a decision. Clem is the priority for both of us right now.'

Thoughts of what to do churned through her head. There were no magazines to distract her. Someone had told her they were considered too unhygienic these days to be kept in hospitals and doctors' waiting rooms. She scrolled through her phone but didn't want to run the battery down too much, when she hadn't thought to bring a charger. But one thought prevailed—it was absolutely wonderful having Jon here by her side at such a worrying time.

'Do you remember the night Clem was born?' Jon asked, after they'd sat in silence for what seemed an age.

She put down her phone. 'Only too well, and

being here is bringing it all back. You were there with me.'

'Your mother was furious it was me with you and not her. But the midwife let her know in no uncertain terms that the father had priority.'

She smiled. 'You were so good, feeding me chipped ice, encouraging me.'

'You crushed the bones in my hand every time you had a contraction.'

'You rubbed my back in between. It really helped.'

'I put up with you screaming at me how much you hated me as you pushed.'

'You knew I didn't really mean it.'

'You actually apologised. Until the next command to push and I was the villain again for getting you into the situation.'

'Don't listen to anyone who says childbirth isn't painful,' she said ruefully.

'Then we both shed tears of joy when they put that perfect, tiny, red-faced person on your tummy,' he said.

'Together we counted her fingers and toes.'

'We couldn't stop looking at her.'

'She was a miracle. I couldn't believe I'd grown that precious treasure inside me.'

'We bonded with her instantly.'

'And I loved you even more for making her with me,' she said.

Jon smiled. 'I didn't think I could love you any more than I already did but I found another level of love for the mother of my baby.'

'And it's that grown-up baby who my life still revolves around,' Natalie said. 'Her, and now her baby.'

Love. They spoke so casually about it. Because that was in the past. Could she love Jon again? She silently chastised herself. She already loved him. She'd fallen back in love with him so easily. When? She couldn't pinpoint it. The love was just there again.

'The C-section must be quite a different experience,' said Jon.

'Not what she wanted, but all that matters is that she and the baby are okay.'

'Yes,' he said. 'And all we can do is wait.'

CHAPTER FIFTEEN

WAITING, WAITING, WAITING. Natalie had no idea whether Clem was still awaiting surgery, was actually in the operating theatre, or was in recovery. And the baby? They'd already been there an hour. Jon had gone to the downstairs café for a coffee and brought her back a magazine that didn't catch her interest. She hadn't wanted a coffee. The thought of it made her gag.

There were a number of people in the waiting room, including Tyler's parents, who'd not long arrived. She'd greeted them briefly, but now they were huddled together, not wanting to talk. She looked around to keep herself distracted. There were some interesting faces. She passed some time thinking about how she might paint their portraits.

Then an altogether different young man swept into the waiting room and caught her eye. Very tall, black-haired, self-assured, extremely good-looking, wearing a superbly cut dark brown wool coat. Italian perhaps? He looked as if he'd stepped off the pages of a European fashion magazine. Where did he belong? Was he a doctor? A consultant? Or an expectant father?

The man exchanged a few words with the midwife behind the desk. She led him away, but a few minutes later he returned. Then, to her surprise, the man walked towards them. Was this Leo?

He stopped in front of her chair, hand outstretched. 'Jon? Natalie? I'm Leo Constello, Clem's partner. I'm the man who hopes to marry your daughter. You are Clementine's mother?'

'Why, yes,' she said.

'I thought as much, you look so like her.' He turned to Jon. 'And you must be her father. The same eyes.'

'That's right,' said Jon, obviously a little bemused by this model-gorgeous, charismatic man.

'It's wonderful that you managed to get here,' Natalie said, a little numbly. 'We wondered where you were.'

'I got here as fast as I could once the midwife told me what had happened,' Leo said.

Natalie exchanged a glance with Jon. Leo wanted to marry Clem? How did they not know this?

'That's very good of you,' Jon said.

Leo smiled. 'I know we've not been seeing each other long, but I love Clem and I will be the father of her baby.'

Leo smiled and Natalie caught her breath at just how incredibly attractive he was. If Leo was speaking the truth, and he and Clem were in love and committed to one another and this baby going forward, Clem was one lucky woman.

'Clem didn't tell you too much about us because I think she still had doubts that I would want to take on another man's child. But I assure you, I will treat her baby as if he or she were my own. You can trust me on that.'

'That's good to know,' said Natalie, still struggling to believe what she was hearing.

'Natalie, I really do love your daughter very much. I haven't asked her to marry me yet, but I intend to propose as soon as I can and convince her I mean it. Nothing would make me happier than to have Clem as my wife. I will love her and cherish both her and our baby for the rest of our lives.'

'That's wonderful news, Leo,' Natalie said.

She wasn't sure about hugging him, so settled for a hand on his arm. 'Congratulations. As you know, Clem is an exceptional person in every way. Not that I am biased as her mother.'

Leo smiled. 'I know just how exceptional Clem is—but I admit to being biased as I both love and admire her.'

A perfect answer, Natalie thought, pleased.

'That will make me your father-in-law,' said Jon, shaking Leo's hand again.

Was there an undertone from Jon of *and you'd better look after my little girl or you'll have me to answer to*? Natalie couldn't be sure, but she secretly smiled.

Just then Clem's midwife called them all over to the desk. 'Clementine's surgery has gone well. Her baby will be taken straight to our neonatal ICU.' She paused and the pause seemed ominous. Natalie's heart sank to the tip of her boots. 'Clementine is unconscious. We'll let you know when she comes to.'

'Unconscious? What does that mean?' Natalie's knees gave way under her. She was grateful for Jon's immediate support.

'It's because of the eclampsia,' the midwife said. 'Rest assured she is being monitored, all her signs are good, and we expect a full recovery.' She turned to Leo. 'I will take you to see the baby now.'

Natalie stepped forward. The midwife put up her hand. 'Clementine's partner only at this stage,' she said. 'As he's listed as the next of kin.'

Leo shot her a sympathetic glance. 'I'll be back with a full report when I can,' he said as he followed the midwife out of sight.

'You okay?' said Jon, supporting her by the elbow.

'I think so,' she said. 'But I need to sit down.' Jon led her back to her seat.

'Take a moment to recover from the shock,' he said.

'Which one? The fact Clem is unconscious after giving birth to a premature baby or the fact that she's apparently going to marry Leo? It's almost too much to take in.'

'Leo seems like a good guy,' Jon said. 'I liked him. Let me look him up.'

Jon whipped out his phone and scanned his screen, nodding as he read. 'Yep, he's ideal. Brilliant academic record. Meteoric rise in the bank. From an extremely wealthy family. Single. Never been married or divorced. A good catch for our Clem.'

Our Clem. Natalie liked the way Jon said

that. 'Did you just call that gorgeous, sophisticated young man a "good catch" for our daughter?'

'He's getting an equally good catch,' Jon said with a grin. 'Or shall I just say, they seem well matched?'

'Clem has never had anything but praise for him as her boss.' Natalie took a deep breath. 'But she hardly talked about him on a personal level, so, despite him moving in with her recently, I had no idea how serious they really were about each other.'

'It's what he said. It must have been tricky for both of them to fall in love while she's pregnant with another man's baby. The fact Tyler died probably only made it trickier. I should imagine they've had their ups and downs, but he seemed genuinely in love to me.'

'Clem is my daughter. I should have guessed how she was feeling.'

'How could you have? And how disappointed you would have been if it hadn't worked out for them. If Leo had decided to walk away in the end, because he didn't want to bring up another man's child. I mean, Hugo did it, full credit to him. The brutal truth is not every man would,' Jon said. 'Clem did the right thing not telling us too much. And besides, it's actually none of our business.'

'You're right. But he'll be family. Our family. So, it is kind of our business.'

'He seemed respectful. And I liked the way he made it so clear how much he loves Clem and that his intentions are honourable.'

Natalie smiled. 'That's an old-fashioned turn of phrase.'

'You know what I mean,' Jon said with an answering smile.

'I also like that he's not afraid to declare his love for and commitment to Clem,' Natalie said.

'Not only will we be grandparents but we'll also be parents-in-law.'

Natalie took his hand. 'Family. Our family,' she said. 'But not knowing she and Leo were in love… It…it stings somewhat. Clem excluding me from something so important, I mean.'

'Like we're excluding her from our story?'

'I guess. Though it's not really the same, is it?'

'I think what's stinging most is that you're no longer needed like you thought you were going to be.'

She sighed. 'You could be right.'

'Leo gets to see the baby first. Not you. No

doubt it will be Leo sitting by Clem's bedside. Not you. She will have a husband soon, by the sound of it, and their first priority will be to each other and their child.'

'As it should be.'

'You don't sound completely convinced.'

She sighed again. 'I… I think I'm just feeling surplus to requirements.'

Jon let a beat go by before he answered. 'Of course you're not. Clem has Leo now and a life with him to look forward to. That doesn't mean she won't still need her mum. Especially for help with the baby.'

'You're right. It's just a lot to be hit with at the same time. She'll be a mother, a bride, a wife. Leo will be part of the family. Usually those kinds of life stages happen one after the other, in order. Not all at once.'

'I think it's great, after all she's been through. Leo seems a strong kind of guy and protective. That's what a father wants for his daughter. He can give her a good life.'

'I know you're right. I… I just wasn't prepared for this quite yet.'

'It is unexpected. Especially when you've been so geared up to looking after her. But part of loving Clem is to let her spread her wings and fly—even if that's away from you.'

'I know you're right. It's just…'

'And a tip from a former despised son-in-law? Make a friend of Leo. Don't exclude him. Everyone's life will be happier.'

She nodded. 'I absolutely know you're right. I suspect there's a reason Clem has kept me on the periphery of her life with Leo—because she doesn't want me going all overprotective on her.'

'It works both ways, you know. For you, I mean. Your wings have been clipped for a long time. Fitting Hugo's idea of a wife must have been an effort—well, that's my reading of it, correct me if I'm wrong. You've put Clem first at all times. Tried to placate your parents. Kissed goodbye to a career. It's your turn to spread your wings and soar now. Soar as high and far as you want to.'

'Straight into your arms?'

'If that's the direction you choose to fly.'

'Flap my newly freed wings and fly towards Perth?'

He laughed. 'It's a very long way. But migrating birds do it.'

'Then maybe I can too.' She smiled.

'Leo's role in Clem's life has changed the dynamic. You can plan a life of your own now. Think carefully about what you want.'

What did she want? For the first time in her life Natalie actually had a choice about what she wanted from life. Right back from when she'd fallen pregnant with Clem, other people had made choices for her—her parents, Hugo, Jon. And then she'd chosen to put Clem first.

The other night she'd told Clem she didn't want to get tied down to a man again—but now there was Jon. She was loving being with him, never more so than this time here at the hospital with trauma swirling around them and he proving to be her rock. It was all very well to have the freedom to make her own choices, but what if the life she wanted would be all the sweeter for having the man she had always loved by her side? Could they make it work a second time, this time bonded not only by their feelings for each other but also by their connection to Clem and her new little family? Reigniting their relationship was taking a risk, Jon had said. Was she ready to risk her heart again?

'You have time to really think about what you want, Natalie,' Jon said. 'Especially about what you want from me.'

'I know I want—'

At that moment a midwife came into the waiting room. 'All seems well with the baby.

Clementine is still unconscious and her partner is in the NICU with the baby.'

Natalie's first impulse was to ask if she could go and sit by Clem's bedside. But she didn't. That was now Leo's place. Besides, she didn't want to suffer the humiliation of being told that by the midwife.

'You can all see the baby in the NICU now if you'd like,' the midwife said.

'Yes, please,' said Natalie with a flutter of excitement.

'Each set of grandparents, one at a time,' the midwife added.

Natalie held her breath in awe at her first sight of Clem's baby. The tiny person, born five and a half weeks early, was lying in an incubator attached to what seemed to be a mass of wires and tubes. Natalie's eyes misted over at the sight. Was that a faint fuzz of ginger hair she saw—or was she imagining it?

'Is my grandbaby okay?' she asked the midwife.

'For how long will the incubator be needed?' Jon asked.

'Baby is a good weight, strong and doing well. As soon as baby can breathe unassisted, the tubes will be taken out.'

Natalie wasn't allowed to touch the baby or

get too close, but she knew Jon was visually counting fingers and toes as she was. She had to take the midwife's word that all was well.

'And my daughter?'

'We don't know for how long she'll be unconscious. Do you live far?'

'Quite close by,' said Jon.

'Then I suggest you go home. I'll call you when Clementine wakes up.'

'No,' Natalie said.

'No,' Jon said at the same time.

'We'll be in the waiting room,' Natalie said. We won't be going home until we see our daughter.'

CHAPTER SIXTEEN

IT WAS A very long wait for both Natalie and Jon, as well as Tyler's parents Fiona and Gary, who joined them in the waiting room not long after they'd seen the baby. Natalie was glad they'd been allowed to see the baby too, and it was a highly emotional time for them, although they'd relaxed now that the baby was fine and wanted to chat. Natalie didn't attempt to discuss Leo's presence with them, but it wasn't hard to see that Leo was important to Clem. That would be Clem's job for later. She was happy to introduce Jon as Clem's birth father and mention that they were friends and on good terms.

Finally, eight hours after she'd given birth, Clem woke up. The midwife told the waiting grandparents that Leo and the baby had been by her side when she'd opened her eyes. The hospital had run more tests on her and she'd been given the all-clear.

When Natalie finally saw her daughter in her private room, she was shocked at how pale Clem looked, lying back on the hospital bed. But also how happy and contented. Clem's baby lay sleeping angelically in a high clear plastic bassinet on wheels by the side of the bed.

'Oh, sweet pea, what an adventure,' Natalie said, taking her daughter's hand. 'I don't dare hug you as I know you've got stitches.'

'Feeling very tender,' Clem said. 'But I'm so ecstatic about the baby I'm not feeling much pain. Though that might be the painkillers they've given me. Leo tells me you guys were waiting out there all day. Thank you.'

'Is there something you want to tell us about Leo?' Natalie asked with a not-so-subtle raising of her eyebrows.

'You'll hear all about that later, Mum.' Clem looked up at her father. 'But I think you and Dad have some explaining to do.'

'Who? Us?' said Jon, but his mock innocence wasn't convincing. Especially as he was holding Natalie's hand.

'You'll hear all about me and Jon later,' said Natalie. She was careful not to commit to anything. Especially as she and Jon hadn't actually committed to anything. There was still a chance this thing with Jon could be only a fling.

Clem smiled. 'I think I can see what's happening, but I'll let you play parent-style games if it amuses you.'

'Sweet pea, the midwife told me you and the baby won't be discharged until Christmas Eve, six days away. What do you want me to do at the town house for your Christmas Day dinner? You know I've got a key.'

'I've ordered most of the food for delivery or pick up. I'll give you a list when I'm feeling more like myself. As you know, I put up the tree and the decorations at the very end of October.'

'Don't worry, I'll get it sorted and buy in any extra food we might need, fresh fruit and veg and so on. Jon lives quite close to Borough Market, so we can shop there.'

Clem's knowing smile made Natalie realise she had given her—and Jon—away to her perceptive daughter. 'How convenient for you, Mum. You're staying at Dad's apartment, are you? I wasn't sure if you'd decided—'

'It actually is more convenient for visiting you here, sweet pea.'

'Sure it is,' said Clem, knowingly.

'Our five minutes' allocated visiting time is

up,' Natalie said. 'The nurse will be bustling in here in a minute to kick us out.'

'Thanks, Mum, for everything. And you too, Dad.'

'It's what parents do,' said Natalie. 'We'll see you tomorrow, sweet pea, in visiting hours. Call if you need me to bring anything for you.'

Jon followed Natalie out of Clem's room. How easily he and Natalie had slipped into the role of husband and wife, concerned parents, worried grandparents. He liked it. He wanted it to be for real. But he and Natalie had to be sure it was what she wanted—and how they could achieve it.

When, on the way down to the hospital lobby, they reached a relatively quiet stretch of corridor, he turned to Natalie and stopped her with a hand on her arm. 'Where to? My apartment? Or do you want me to drive you home to Guildford?'

'Do you want me to come to yours?'

'Of course I do. We did plan for you to stay until Christmas Day. We can go down and get Freddie tomorrow, if that suits.'

'I want to stay with you.' She took a deep breath. 'I haven't changed my mind about wanting to be with you. Long-term, I mean.'

'I haven't changed my mind about wanting you with me, long-term.'

'As you said, Clem marrying Leo does change the dynamic. She won't need me as much. Oh, maybe for the first few months with the baby, but I suspect Leo will want to be a hands-on dad. Then, as you said, I can claim my own life back. The life I want is to be with you. My wings are limbering up for a flight straight to you, wherever you are in the world.'

Jon cupped his hand under her chin so she looked up at him. She had never looked more beautiful, even with smeared make-up and weary shadows under her eyes. 'In that interminable wait in that uncomfortable waiting room, I thought a lot about what you'd said— and that was before Leo told us he wanted to marry Clem. Of course a FIFO arrangement wasn't going to work for us, certainly not for that long-term. We would both hate it. I was asking you to do all the compromising. I've been too rigid, too obsessive in my no-end-in-sight quest for more and more wealth. But I'd be bored if I retired.'

'So what do you intend to do?'

'Wind back on some of the travel to out-of-the-way mine sites. Streamline my business so I can work remotely much of the time. I left England for us. Now I'm prepared to come back to England for us. Have more time for you, basically. You are more important to me than anything else.'

'Really?' Her voice hitched on the word.

'You and Clem. All the drama of today—we could have lost both Clem and her baby—made me focus on what's really important. The people we love. And I love you, Natalie. I've always loved you. I've never loved anyone else.'

Her eyes gleamed. 'I love you too, Jon. I loved you from the moment I saw you playing guitar way back in Durham. We went through tough times. I thought I hated you there for a while but only because you'd hurt me so much. I felt guilty because I couldn't love Hugo—I realise now that was because there was no room in my heart because you were already there.'

He kissed her, short but very sweet—after all, they were in the corridor of a busy hospital.

Natalie took a deep breath. 'I think if Hugo were still alive now, and I met you again like this, I would have left him to be with you.'

'I wouldn't have asked that of you.' *Although he stole you from me and it would only have been fair.*

'I know,' she said. 'But the reality is we're

both free to love each other again without answering to anyone.'

'Or hurting anyone,' he added.

'We can live our lives the way we choose to. And that looks like it might be living between two countries and some other travel in between.'

'Including side trips to Florence and France for your painting classes.'

'That too. Maybe painting portraits of some Australian dogs.'

'Whatever you want it to be.'

'I don't want to live in the Guildford house. But I want to keep it for Clem, if she wants it.'

'That sounds like a plan. I'll buy us a house with a garden for Freddie and our grandchild. Somewhere not far from where Clem and Leo end up living and not too far from Heathrow.'

'We'll have fun looking for that. Will you keep the Waterloo apartment?'

'Of course. We'll need a city house. You'll like the Perth house too. It's right on the Swan River with a pool and lots of room. It's a beautiful house, but it needs a heart. You'll bring that to it.'

She tucked her arm through his. 'C'mon, let's go home to Waterloo.' She looked up to him. 'You do realise that, from now on, wherever you are will be home to me.'

'I like that. Same for me with you.'

They took the elevator to the hospital lobby. As the doors opened, they were greeted by the sounds of a choir singing Christmas carols. Turned out it was the hospital choir. Natalie looked to him in delight. 'How perfect. And listen, they're singing "God Rest Ye Merry, Gentlemen" just for you.'

'How thoughtful of them,' he said, holding her close as they listened.

He had never felt happier, even happier than when they'd been together and in love as teen-agers. Now they had a daughter and a grand-child and a soon-to-be son-in-law and the prospect of a fulfilling life together stretch-ing ahead of them. They deserved this second chance at love. They listened to the choir sing 'We Wish You a Merry Christmas' before turn-ing to each other and deciding to go home. It had been a very long and traumatic day.

It was dark outside as they exited the hospital doors. And very cold. Natalie lifted her face up to the sky. 'Snow,' she said in awe. 'It's snowing.' Flurries of fat snowflakes drifted and danced down through the darkness and hospital lights towards them. There was a light white cover on the ground and the tops of nearby parked cars. Christmas music drifted from the lobby. 'How magical,' she breathed. 'Snow for Christmas. Snow for the birth of our grandbaby.'

'Snow for the woman I love,' he said and kissed her. 'Natalie, there is one more thing I want to say before we head for the car.'

'Go ahead,' she said.

'Will you marry me? Marry me again, I mean.'

'Yes,' she said straight away. 'Nothing could make me happier than to marry you. Marry you again, that is. Will that make me your third wife?' she teased.

He pulled her close and kissed her. 'Under law, there's no second-chance marriage ceremony, like a renewal of vows,' he said. 'I looked it up. Divorce extinguished our first marriage. We have to start again. So legally, I guess you would be. As well as my first.'

She looked up at him, snowflakes caught on her hair and on her eyelashes. 'That's a good thing, isn't it? To start again? Older and a whole lot wiser and with a family we love? Having made our mistakes and held tight to our second chance to love each other?'

'Yes, a very good thing,' he said, taking hold of her hand and walking with her through the dancing snowflakes and into their new life together.

EPILOGUE

LATE AFTERNOON ON 23 December, Natalie and Jon were at the Kensington town house, finalising the preparations for Christmas Day lunch. All Clem would have to do on Christmas morning was to supervise her parents while they assembled the meal the way she wanted it. It was to be a veritable feast.

They hadn't had to do anything in the way of cleaning and tidying. The place had been immaculate when they'd arrived there this morning. They hadn't had to do any Christmas decorating either. Clem had seen to that.

The decorations were particularly elegant and coordinated, in keeping with Clem's godmother Audrey's exquisite décor. Not like the hodgepodge of mismatched baubles and lights with a bulb missing that made up the family decorations at Guildford. Natalie had brought a lovely sugarplum fairy from the house that

Clem had particularly loved as a little girl and added it to the big tree in the corner of Audrey's living room. She'd also bought a hand-embroidered tapestry Baby's First Christmas stocking to hang on the mantelpiece.

'That's only useful for one year,' Jon said. 'Bit of a waste, isn't it?'

'I suspect Clem and Leo won't stop at one child so it might come in handy another year. Besides, it's the spirit of the thing.'

Then there was the beautiful wreath Jon had bought for Clem at the Covent Garden Christmas market. It sat perfectly on the panelled front door of the town house. 'That will be a lovely surprise for Clem and Leo when they bring the baby home tomorrow,' Natalie said.

Importantly, she and Jon had followed Clem's instructions to get the room allocated as a nursery ready for baby's arrival tomorrow. Everything was there, they just had to put some of it together as Clem hadn't anticipated finalising that until January.

'Shall we go home now?' said Jon.

How quickly Natalie had begun to think of the Waterloo apartment as home. She'd moved into the master bedroom with Jon and had brought up some of the clothes and possessions from the Guildford house. That included enough painting equipment to start the first portrait of her grandbaby. And Freddie, of course.

'One more thing, did you stash your guitar in Audrey's closet?'

'Yes. Our carol singing will remain a secret until we actually get the guitar out on Christmas Day.' He paused. 'I'm still not certain about that. Leo seems a sophisticated kind of guy. We might embarrass Clem.'

'I very much doubt that. Clem is over the moon that we're getting married again. And we sound pretty darn good singing together, even if I do say so myself.'

'Of course we do,' he said, pulling her to him in a hug. 'Everything is set for our family reunion in London.'

She pulled away. 'One final thing. The sequinned Santa hats.'

'Placed in the top drawer of the sideboard, as requested.'

'Good. Wasn't I clever to have got them in time for the baby to appreciate them?'

'You were very clever, although the baby won't notice them,' he said with an indulgent smile followed by a quick kiss.

Natalie laughed. 'Jon, isn't this going to be the best Christmas ever?'

'It's going to be the best life ever, my darling wife-to-be,' he said, pulling her back into his arms where she belonged and kissing her again.

* * * * *

Look out for the next story in the Family Reunion in London duet

Christmas Surprise for Her Boss
by Scarlet Wilson

And if you enjoyed this story, check out these other great reads from Kandy Shepherd

The Tycoon's Christmas Dating Deal
Cinderella and the Tycoon Next Door
Mistletoe Magic in Tahiti

All available now!

Get up to 4 Free Books!

We'll send you 2 free books from each series you try
PLUS a free Mystery Gift.

FREE Value Over **$25**

Both the **Harlequin® Historical** and **Harlequin® Romance** series feature compelling novels filled with emotion and simmering romance.

YES! Please send me 2 FREE novels from the Harlequin Historical or Harlequin Romance series and my FREE Mystery Gift (gift is worth about $10 retail). After receiving them, if I don't wish to receive any more books, I can return the shipping statement marked "cancel." If I don't cancel, I will receive 5 brand-new Harlequin Historical books every month and be billed just $6.39 each in the U.S. or $7.19 each in Canada, or 4 brand-new Harlequin Romance Larger-Print books every month and be billed just $7.19 each in the U.S. or $7.99 each in Canada, a savings of 20% off the cover price. It's quite a bargain! Shipping and handling is just 50¢ per book in the U.S. and $1.25 per book in Canada.* I understand that accepting the 2 free books and gift places me under no obligation to buy anything. I can always return a shipment and cancel at any time by calling the number below. The free books and gift are mine to keep no matter what I decide.

Choose one: ☐ **Harlequin Historical** (246/349 BPA G36Y)   ☐ **Harlequin Romance Larger-Print** (119/319 BPA G36Y)   ☐ **Or Try Both!** (246/349 & 119/319 BPA G36Z)

Name (please print)

Address   Apt. #

City   State/Province   Zip/Postal Code

Email: Please check this box ☐ if you would like to receive newsletters and promotional emails from Harlequin Enterprises ULC and its affiliates. You can unsubscribe anytime.

Mail to the Harlequin Reader Service:
IN U.S.A.: P.O. Box 1341, Buffalo, NY 14240-8531
IN CANADA: P.O. Box 603, Fort Erie, Ontario L2A 5X3

Want to explore our other series or interested in ebooks? Visit www.ReaderService.com or call 1-800-873-8635.

*Terms and prices subject to change without notice. Prices do not include sales taxes, which will be charged (if applicable) based on your state or country of residence. Canadian residents will be charged applicable taxes. Offer not valid in Quebec. This offer is limited to one order per household. Books received may not be as shown. Not valid for current subscribers to the Harlequin Historical or Harlequin Romance series. All orders subject to approval. Credit or debit balances in a customer's account(s) may be offset by any other outstanding balance owed by or to the customer. Please allow 4 to 6 weeks for delivery. Offer available while quantities last.

Your Privacy—Your information is being collected by Harlequin Enterprises ULC, operating as Harlequin Reader Service. For a complete summary of the information we collect, how we use this information and to whom it is disclosed, please visit our privacy notice located at https://corporate.harlequin.com/privacy-notice. Notice to California Residents – Under California law, you have specific rights to control and access your data. For more information on these rights and how to exercise them, visit https://corporate.harlequin.com/california-privacy. For additional information for residents of other U.S. states that provide their residents with certain rights with respect to personal data, visit https://corporate.harlequin.com/other-state-residents-privacy-rights/.

HHHRLP25